Trapped in H

Chapter 1

Maggie

I woke up with a throbbing headache, disoriented and groggy. Where was I? My surroundings were unfamiliar, and I struggled to remember how I had ended up in this situation. The room was dimly lit, and my limbs felt heavy, like I'd been drugged or something. With great effort, I tried to gather my wits and assess my surroundings, searching for any clues that might lead to my escape, but I was clueless.

I was trapped, my wrists bound tightly with rough, coarse rope. The musty smell of the damp, oppressive air hung heavy in the space. Fear and anxiety coursed through me as I realized that I was still being held captive. The room offered no escape, and the distant sound of waves suggested I was near water.

Before I could make sense of the situation, I heard two sets of footsteps and voices approaching. Not wanting to show the captors that I was awake, I turned to my side and clenched my eyes shut. My heart raced, and an icy shiver ran down my spine as an overwhelming sense of fear took hold. But nevertheless, my plan for being asleep seemed to work because I was left undisturbed.

"*Tā xǐngle ma*?" **(She awake yet?)**

I recognized Kang's voice straight away.

It was as if a thousand butterflies had turned to lead in my stomach, making it difficult to breathe.

I was with them.

The Jinyoung brothers.

Fuck!

They'd taken me. Again.

Once again, I was held against my will.

Once again, I was their captive.

Slowly, the realisation began to sink in, like a lead weight pulling me deeper into despair - I might never escape this seemingly endless nightmare. The walls of my confinement, both literal and figurative closed in on me, and the hope of ever breaking free began to fade like a distant dream, leaving me with an unshakeable sense of hopelessness.

"*Tā hěn kuài jiù huì xǐng lái*, **(She will be awake soon)** and when she does you will need to be alert brother. There is no room for fuck ups."

The second I heard the authority in his voice, it had me shaking in fear. Yuta was terrifying. His presence alone sent shivers down my spine, and I couldn't help but feel an overwhelming sense of dread whenever he fuck you today sadly, but hopefully very soon."

He winced as he dropped his hand and motioned to the tray. "I'm instead here to feed you. It's been more than twenty-four hours since you were last fed. You must be hungry?"

I looked from his shoulder wound to the food. "I'd rather starve."

Kang lifted the lid off the plate, revealing eggs on toast. God, it looked good, but no doubt they'd done something to it. I wasn't stupid.

He held the fork in front of my mouth. "Open."

I answered him with a glare.

He sighed. "Open your mouth before I shove my cock in there."

Without a word, I took my free hand and pushed the tray off the night-stand, the food splattering everywhere. Kang scrambled off the bed, his nostrils flaring and threw the fork he had in his grasp at me. Thankfully, it missed my head by an inch.

"Don't ever do something like that again." Kang growled.

"I'm not hungry." I said simply.

Kang growled as he touched his shoulder. "Fucking starve then, bitch!"

I growled in frustration. “Just let me go!”

He studied me and grinned as he clambered back onto the bed on top of me, his arms on either side of my head. “Not even a please?”

With my free hand, I try to reach for his neck to strangle him but he slaps it away. “Please, let me go!”

He ran his nose along my jaw and whispered. “Why should I? Huh?”

“I just want to go home.” I whispered.

He stuttered mockingly. “But you can’t.”

“If you don’t let me go now, someone will eventually come for me.”

Staring at my lips, he leans down within an inch of touching them. “Whoever decides to come for you, they don’t have a chance in hell of finding you.”

“You’re wrong.”

He frowned. “You really think someone’s coming for you, don’t you?”

I thrusted my chin up. “My father will come. I know he will.”

He scoffed. “You think daddy’s going to come for you? You haven’t got a chance in hell to be fucking found.”

I sighed in annoyance. “Just let me go now and I’ll

forget this all ever happened."

Kang pouted. "But with you gone, I won't have anyone to play with."

"I'm not anyone's plaything, let alone yours." I snarled.

He smirked. "After last time, I think it's safe to say that you are. Yuta and I loved playing with you. We can't wait for round two."

I spat on the floor. "Fuck you and your brother."

"You have. More than once." With a soft and quick kiss, he clambers off and gazes out the window.

With the back of my free hand, I wiped my lips and grimaced. "It's not like I had a choice."

"And it will continue to be like that. We're here."

I widened my eyes. "Where?"

"Your new home." He turned around, looked at the mess on the floor and chuckled. "Welcome to Hong Kong, whore."

Chapter 2

Maggie

A few minutes after Kang left the room, the boat came to a stop. As I waited, nervousness gripped me tightly. My heart raced, and my palms grew moist. Thoughts swirled in my mind, like a turbulent storm, and self-doubt whispered in my ear. I tried to take deep breaths to calm myself, but the knot in my stomach remained. The anticipation of what was waiting for me outside was overwhelming. Yet, beneath the nervousness, a spark of excitement flickered. This could be my only chance to escape from this hell, and prove to myself that I could overcome this fear. I could try and make a run for it as soon as I touch land, or scream and hope somebody would hear me…I shook my head. No. Don't be stupid, Maggie. Nobody would help me. Not here. Not in the place where the Jinyoung's ruled their empire.

Suddenly, my door unexpectedly opened, causing me to wake up from my stupor. When I see who it is, I immediately tense up. Yuta walked in carrying a bundle of clothes in his hands. When I looked up at him, his face held no expression as he came to a stop at the end of the bed.

As much as I hated to admit it, Yuta was striking. His features were both beautiful and intense. His eyes were dark and penetrating, holding a depth of emotion that was impossible to ignore. He seemed to have the power to see right through me. His skin was a flawless canvas, with an arrogant and confident complexion that drew you in. His hair was jet-black and meticulously styled, adding an air of sophistication to his overall look. What truly set him apart was his aura of intensity. He had a magnetic presence, and every word he spoke carried weight and purpose. It was as though he possessed an inner fire, a burning passion that made him truly captivating. In his presence, I couldn't help but feel the powerful energy he radiated, and it left a lasting impression.

He dropped the clothes on the bed and came towards me. He then reached inside one of his pockets and pulled out a single, silver key. He roughly grabbed my wrist, put the key inside the cuff and with a click, I was free.

Go! Now, Maggie!

"Don't." Yuta warned.

"Don't do what?" I asked.

He raised a brow. "Run."

My shoulders sagged. "What gave you that impression?" I pulled my wrist back, and stroked the tender lesion caused by the tight cuff.

"I could see it in your face. Don't even try it."

Anyone would have had the same idea if they were kept against their will.

"Do you really think you were going to get far? Armed guards are all over the place and won't hesitate to shoot you."

Maybe that wouldn't be such a bad thing…

"Whore?"

I tensed my jaw, but didn't acknowledge him.

"You think ignoring me is going to make this whole situation better for you?"

Yes.

"Fine. Keep ignoring me and see just how quickly I get pissed off."

"*Hal mal-i eobsda.*" **(I have nothing to say)** I uttered.

Reaching out, he grabbed my chin and pulled it up to his face. "You've got nothing to say to me? Good, because that makes the two of us. Now, get out of those clothes. You stink."

As soon as he let me go, I grabbed the first thing I saw which was a gray shirt dress that fell just above my knees, and a pair of black pumps. No bra. And no underwear. Just to make sure that they weren't hiding amongst the pile of clothes, I rummaged through them only to come up empty-handed.

"There's no underwear." I murmured.

He sighed. "And you won't find any."

I looked at him in question.

He shrugged. "You won't be needing them."

"Why?"

Yuta smirked. "You never know when I might want to fuck you."

I grimaced. "I'd rather be punished than have anything to do with you."

His face hardened. "Be careful what you wish for because in this world, even looking at someone the wrong way can get you punished or worse killed."

I stayed silent.

He continued. "But with that tongue of yours, I'm not sure if you'll even survive a day in the hell that awaits you."

Again, I stayed silent.

Yuta raised a brow. "Really? Nothing to say? Nothing at all? Could it be that you're finally accepting the fact that this is your life?"

Absolutely not. I would never accept this life.

He waits for me to speak, but when nothing comes out he chuckles. “You can listen, after all. Too bad you couldn’t be this obedient back in America.”

Yuta sauntered over to me and grabbed me by the upper arm, pulling me towards the door. “Now, from this moment on you’ll call me and every man you see, sir. Understood?”

When I don’t respond he gives my arm a sharp tug. “Don’t test my patience, Maggie. I asked you if you understood?”

“Yes, sir.” I said through gritted teeth.

He searched my eyes. “Before we reach our destination, there are a few rules I must tell you. Whether or not you listen to them will be entirely up to you. The first rule. Do not make any eye contact unless you are instructed to do so and the second rule is, do not speak unless you’re spoken to. Break any of these rules, you will be punished. Are we understood?”

Fuck. You.

“Yes, sir.”

Anger burned inside of me at the mention of that word. When did I become so weak? This wasn't like me at all. I should lash out, kick him, punch him, anything other than being told what to do. This wasn't who I was born to be, and just as I dug my heels into

home. The colour palette was a harmonious blend of soft pastels, with shades of blush pink, powder blue, and mint green. The walls were painted a warm, inviting cream colour, which set the perfect backdrop for the decor. Large, arched windows let in an abundance of natural light, and the sheer curtains swayed gently in the breeze. The wooden floors were polished to a high shine and covered with plush, ivory-coloured area rugs that invited you to take off your shoes and sink your feet into its softness. The furniture was a mix of classic and modern pieces, with a comfortable and stylish sofa in a delicate shade of grey. A vintage chandelier hung from the ceiling, casting a soft, warm glow over the room. The walls were adorned with elegant framed artwork and mirrors that reflected the room's beauty. Fresh flowers and potted plants were strategically placed around the room, adding a touch of nature and vibrancy. A grand piano sat in one corner, waiting to be played, while a cosy reading nook with a plush armchair and a small bookshelf beckoned you to relax and unwind. The kitchen, a chef's dream, boasted sleek granite countertops, stainless steel appliances, and an expansive island with barstools for casual dining.

Only then did I notice the four half-naked girls sitting at the dining room table eating breakfast. Each of them looked at me curiously. I took in one particular Asian girl who had enormous breasts. They were so big that if she leant forward, her breasts could rest on the table.

Mine were quite big but hers were ridiculously large. A long glance at her breasts had me guessing that they were fake. They were too high up and too firm to be real, but she wore them well with her perfect posture.

"This is Maggie." Kang introduced me. "She's from Korea."

The girl with the fake boobs raises her hand and waves at me. "*Sae yeoja annyeonghaseyo.*" **(Hello, new girl)**

"Hi." I murmured.

Kang took hold of my arm and led me to the right side of the room. Comfortable looking beds with elegant, matching bedding sat in rows, each with its own side table and lamp. A vibrant, handwoven rug covered the floor, adding a pop of colour to the room. Personal touches, like framed photos adorned the walls, reflecting the unique personalities of my new roommates.

"The last one's yours." Kang pointed to the very last bed and grinned. "Welcome home."

"Screw you."

Kang digs his nails into my arm. "Didn't Yuta inform you of the do's and don't's here? Unless you want to get punished, I suggest you remember every single fucking detail my brother told you. We're not in America anymore, shits different here. The sooner you accept that, the better it will be for you."

I grunted. "*Jeoldae.*" **(Never)**

He cups my cheek roughly and smiles evilly down at me. "Stop fighting against me, I'm trying to help you."

I frowned, when the girl with the fake boobs joins us and bows when she sees Kang. She even blushes a little bit. Moving away from me, Kang pulled the girl up against his chest, growled and slammed his lips down against hers. Their lips met fervently, hands exploring each other's bodies, and their bodies pressed closely together.

Breathless, the whore smiled as they broke away from one another. "Good afternoon, sir."

"Where are the others?" Kang demanded, stroking the girl's cheek.

The girl smiled sweetly. "They are still with customers. They shouldn't be too long."

"And… Shuang?"

"She was called very early this morning to serve a customer. I have not seen her since she departed her quarters." The girl answered.

I watched his reaction and frowned when I saw him tensing his jaw and his hands fisted at his sides.

What was that about?

"Who… was she serving?" Kang asked.

“The retired man who used to be your father’s bodyguard, sir.”

“Sal?”

The girl nodded.

Rubbing his forehead, Kang motioned to me. “Escort Maggie to the kitchen for some food and then to the showers. Oh, and dress her in white for tonight.”

The girl bowed. “Yes, sir.”

Kang turned to me and stared deeply into my eyes. “You’re in our territory now. Fuck up and you’re dead meat.”

And without a backward glance, he leaves.

“Asshole.” I murmured under my breath.

The girl in front of me cleared her throat and smiled softly. “Welcome. My name is Ling.”

I politely introduced myself. “Maggie.”

“Welcome to Paradise, Maggie.”

Are you fucking kidding me?

I spluttered. “Paradise? Really? That’s what you call this place? Are you high?”

She chuckled. “You are funny.” She motioned to the kitchen. “Come. It is time for lunch. We must do what sir tells us to do.”

"I'd rather not." I muttered as I followed Ling as she walked back the way we came, when I noticed a huge walk-in closet. As I stepped inside, I was surrounded by neatly organised racks of clothing, shoes and accessories. The closet was well-lit, warm lighting, creating a welcoming ambience. On one side, there were rows of clothing rods that displayed a vast array of garments, from elegant dresses and tailored suits to casual wear, all meticulously organised by type and colour. The soft rustle of fabric as I moved through the space was almost like a whisper of fashion possibilities. Shoes shelves lined the opposite wall, showcasing an impressive collection of footwear, from stilettos to sneakers. Mirrors and dressing areas were strategically placed for outfit coordination and checking one's appearance. Drawers and cubbies held neatly folded clothes, small accessories, and jewellery. In the centre of the closet, an island with marble countertop served as a hub for accessories, with jewellery organisers, perfume bottles, and a display of designer handbags.

"Is there any underwear here?" I asked nobody in particular.

"No."

I felt a wave of disappointment wash over me at the truth in Yuta's words, followed Ling out of the closet into the kitchen. I picked the nearest thing I could reach, which turned out to be a bowl of fresh cut strawberries. My heart sank as I thought back to the time, I was lounging in the hot sun by the pool eating strawberries after training the night before. Seemed like a long time ago.

Afterwards, Ling takes me into the shared bathroom. It was a haven of modern convenience and comfort. Sleek, white subway tiles lined the walls, contrasting beautifully with the dark wood cabinetry and marble countertops. A large mirror stretched above a dual sink vanity, well-lit to ensure the girls could get ready with ease. The spacious shower area featured a glass door and a rainforest shower head, and a separate bathtub invited relaxation with a view of the garden outside. A shelf filled with neatly organised towers, toiletries, and potted plants added a touch of personality to the space.

Ling begins to strip and saunters over to the shower without a care in the world. She motions for me to do the same, but I was hesitant.

"Do not be shy." Ling reassured me.

I exhaled and shook my head.

"Come on, shy one." A feminine voice says from behind me. Hands grab the bottom of my dress and lift it effortlessly over my head. "You must be the new girl everyone is talking about."

I turned around and gasped at the beauty of the girl in

front of me. “Who are you?”

Her porcelain skin was flawless, and glowed with a natural radiance. She had expressive almond-shaped eyes, deep and mysterious, adorned with long, dark lashes. Her eyebrows were delicately arched, framing her eyes perfectly. Her features were elegantly sculpted, with high cheekbones and a soft, graceful jawline. Her full, rosy lips curved into a captivating smile that revealed a set of pearly-white teeth. Long sleek black hair cascaded down her back, and the way it caught the light gave it a lustrous shine.

Before she could answer me, Ling addressed the woman. “Shuang! You are back.”

Shuang smiled. “That I am.” She looked from me to the showers. “Come, you must bathe before tonight.”

The woman known as Shuang joined Ling and washed. I crossed my arms over my chest and pressed my legs together. I felt awkward just standing naked and watching them showering, so I did the best I could to swallow my pride and walked over to them.

“How was your customer, Shuang?” Ling asked.

Shuang blushed slightly as she ran her hands over her long, black hair. “This time, I did not have to fake my pleasure.”

Ling chuckled next to me. “Was he better than you know who?”

I looked over at Ling to see her wiggling her brows at Shuang.

Shuang sighed. "Nobody will be better than him."

Who were they talking about?

I quickly lathered my hand with soap, ran it through my blue hair and rinsed it under the hot water. After rinsing off all the soap, I turned off the shower and dried off with a towel. Wrapping myself in the towel, the three of us walked into the lounge where I heard feminine voices. Three women standing in the kitchen area, staring blankly at me.

What now?

I stared back at them and gave them a blank look back. One woman had caramel skin with a red bob and dark brown eyes. Another who had bright blonde hair, tall and wore a blue one-piece corset with white thigh high boots, and another woman with a small, delicate frame with brown hair down to her waist. She wore only a black thong.

"You're the new girl?" The girl with the red bob asked in a strong American voice.

"Yeah." I uttered.

She scoffed. "Welcome to Hell, honey."

Ling tutted. "Come on, girls. Please make Maggie feel welcome."

In unison, the three girls rolled their eyes at me.

"Okay, then." I chuckled, as I shouldered past them, making my way into the walk-in closet with Ling and Shuang hot on my heels.

"Ignore them. Your beauty intimidates them." Shuang explained.

"I get it, I'm hot." I mutter sarcastically.

"That you are." Ling says as she passes me a white one-piece corset, white knee-high socks, and black stilettos. "Here."

Without another word exchanged, I dressed and noticed Ling and Shuang nod in satisfaction at my chest. I looked down and grimaced when I saw my boobs pushed upwards and a lot of cleavage showing.

Fuck this. There was no way in hell I was wearing this.

Just when I went to take it off, Ling chuckled and pushed me onto a stool to do my hair while Shuang did my makeup. Ling gets to work quickly and does my hair up in an elegant chignon while Shuang powders me, blushes me and paints my lips.

"Don't look so unhappy, you look beautiful." Shuang says.

I shudder at the word. No, I looked like a whore.

Without looking at myself in the mirror, I thanked the

girls, stood up only to be met with Yuta.

My heart rate immediately skyrockets because standing in the doorway, with his hands in his pockets, was Yuta. He looked at me, like a predator eyeing its prey.

Yuta tensed his jaw, blinked repeatedly and motioned with his head. “Come with me.”

Shuang puts my feet in a pair of stilettos and hands me a white mask. “Before I forget, this is for tonight.”

I begrudgingly took the mask from her. “Thanks.”

A hand wraps itself around my arm and in a panic I pull away. Yuta gives me a warning look. “Don't fight me.”

“I can't promise that.”

Yuta growled frustratingly. “Maggie...”

I looked up and glared at him. “What?”

“Don’t. Fuck. Up. Especially tonight… please.”

My stomach clenched as I dug my feet deeper into the ground. But when Yuta reached for my arm again, I allowed him to take it.

Chapter 3

Maggie

“Where are you taking me?”

Reluctantly, I found myself being pulled along, footsteps hesitant as I resisted the invisible force guiding me. Every step felt like surrender to the unknown, my surroundings a blur as I’m dragged into a journey I didn’t choose.

“Yuta?”

Yuta hadn’t opened his mouth since taking my arm. Not once. And his silence was unnerving. My heart races, a rapid unease. Thoughts swirl like a tempest in my mind, each one a potential source of worry. Nervousness, a silent companion, tightens its grip, leaving me caught in the delicate balance between anticipation and apprehension.

He ignored me and continued leading me down several corridors.

“...Sir?”

But again, he ignores me.

“Yuta?”

Nothing.

Alright. That's it.

"Fucking answer me!" I shouted.

Suddenly, he swings me around roughly, causing my back to hit the wall hard, and in less than a second, he cages me in with both arms. "What did you just say?"

My chest rises and falls as I gazed into his black, empty eyes. My pulse quickens, not only from the chill of fright but also the electric charge of arousal, creating a complete tapestry where fear and desire intertwined.

Speak, Maggie!

He leant closer to me. "Speak."

I glared at him in return.

He slid his hand underneath one of my thighs. "Answer me otherwise I'm going to fuck you against this wall."

A subtle warmth unfurled within, a quiet awakening that coursed through my veins.

"Is that what you want?" He lifted up my thigh and pressed his hard length against me. "You wanted my attention. Well, you've got it. So, spit it out. The customers are waiting."

Customers.

That word alone seemed to wake me up because this

anger deep inside of me comes from fucking nowhere.

I shoved at his chest, but he didn't move at all. "I am not whoring myself. Not now, not ever."

He looked into both of my eyes, then down at my lips. "You'll do everything I tell you to fucking do."

"Or what?"

He glared down at me. "*Shénme*?" **(What?)**

With a playful glint in my eyes, I placed my hand on top of his, and placed it between my legs, looking up at him seductively. I do it as a way to hopefully change his mind about everything and let me go.

I bit my lip. "What will you do to me if I don't do what you say? Fuck me?"

He wrapped his free hand around my neck and squeezed a little. "I wouldn't fuck you if you were the last woman on Earth. And if you think seducing me out of here will work, don't even bother fucking trying. Now, keep walking."

My shoulders sagged. It was worth a try.

Yuta takes me into a room, the clinical ambience hits me - the antiseptic scent, the white -coated sterility. Fluorescent lights him overhead, casting a clinical glow on stainless steel instruments neatly arranged on trays. The examination table, draped in disposable paper, waits in the centre, a silent witness to countless stories.

"Up." Yuta instructed.

White walls echo with the hushed whispers of health, and the crisp paper on the examination table crinkles beneath me. Yuta walked towards the counter and hastily put on rubber gloves.

My pulse quickened. "*Mwohago issni*?" **(What are you doing?)**

He looked at me. "I'm giving you an exam."

I shrinked back when I noticed a syringe lying among the equipment. "For what?"

He turned towards the medical equipment and peered over at me. "You're getting a shot. Every girl has to have one."

"Why?" I asked.

"A pregnant whore is the last thing we fucking want."

With the cool touch of latex against my skin, the rhythmic beeping of machines, and Yuta's focused gaze created a symphony of sensations. It was a vulnerable moment, stripped down to facts and figures, as the examination unfolded, guided by the pursuit of understanding the intricacies of my body's whispers and murmurs.

A what...?

I stuttered. “Getting pregnant?”

“You’ll be getting a shot every three months, is that clear?”

A baby?

I placed a hand over my stomach. Never in my life had I been put on birth control. Never in my life did I think of having kids. Never in my life did I think I was ever going to have unprotected sex with random men, but that’s the problem with not knowing what waits for you in the future. Anything could happen.

My stomach rolled as I fought the nausea creeping up my throat. The thought of the possibility of becoming pregnant from some random fucking guy made me sick, and for that reason alone, I remained completely still when Yuta injected my arm.

“Maggie?” Yuta says my name in a stern tone. “Is that clear? Stop making me repeat myself and do as you’re told.”

I woke up from my stupor and stared straight forward at the door. “Why should I? It’s not like I’m going to be here forever.”

He frowned.

“I’ll be out of here soon.”

“Oh, really?” He asked amusingly.

“Yes, really. I won’t be needing another shot after this

one."

He ignores me and instead listens to my heart and does all of the checks. He then checked my throat, eyes, nose and my ears before reaching for the syringe. "They'll never find you."

"If that's true then, *naneun yeogiseo beos-eonal geos-ida*." **(I will escape from here)** I said with determination.

He leant forward and whispered in my ear. "You even try to escape this place, I'll shoot your mother and father right between the eyes. With no mercy."

I widened my eyes in outrage. "*Geuge hyeobbag ieoss-eo*!?" **(Was that a threat!?)**

"It is not a threat, it's a warning. You even try to escape this place and the death of your parents will be on your head."

I teared up at the mention of my parents. "Leave my parents out of this."

He leans back and shakes his head. "Threatening their lives is the only way to stop you from escaping and for you to stay put."

"Please."

He tilts his head down. "Then, do as you're told."

I peered up at him. "I don't know… how to be submissive."

“Then, you’ll forever suffer.” Yuta uttered as he injected my arm.

I winced as the tiny sting disrupted the canvas of my skin. “If only Chen were here right now, things would be so different. He’d let me go if I asked him to.”

Yuta chuckled impassively. “If it wasn’t for me, you would’ve died a long time ago.”

Liar.

I frowned. “Chen’s the only reason why I’m still alive.”

Yuta slammed the syringe on the counter and approached me. “Is that what you think?”

“Yes.”

“Chen wasn’t the one who confronted our father about you. I was the one that gave you a second chance to live. Not him. Me! If it wasn’t for that test, your corpse would be rotting in some ditch right now.”

My jaw dropped. “And what?” I leaned forwards and spat into his face. “You think I wanted this!? To be a whore for the rest of my life?”

“Well, you’re alive, aren’t you?”

Silence.

He continued. “And it’s all thanks to me.”

"Just take me home and I’ll forget this ever

happened." I pleaded.

He leaned back and studied me. "Look at you. You've become so desperate and pathetic that some part of me actually pities you."

I didn't need anyone's pity. Let alone his.

"Well, this is what happens when you rob an innocent girl from fucking everything." I motioned to my pathetic state. "This is what you become. Desperate."

He looked at me with a frown for a few seconds, then put away the equipment. Then, without another word, Yuta takes me by the arm and leads me out of the room and through the house. We don't walk very far, but it felt like it. He takes me into a room that looks like a conference room. In the centre of the room was a long table that stretched from one side of the room to the other, with chairs placed tidily underneath.

Yuta points to the chair at the very end. "Tonight, you'll be beside my father. Remember the rules I told you, don't look at him and most of all don't speak to him. You even open your mouth to yawn and it'll be the last thing you ever do." He points to the chair that's at the head of the table. "Go and stand behind his chair, it won't be long until he arrives."

I did as I was told and walked leisurely until I was standing behind Li Wei's chair. I looked around the empty room and wondered if there was anybody watching me. I could feel my legs wanting to make a move, but what if someone caught me? I remember the words Yuta said to me that if I tried to escape, my parents would die. I couldn't let that happen, but what if this was the only chance I was going to get.

I couldn't miss this chance.

Just as I took a couple of steps away from the chair, I saw Shuang making her way towards me in a red corset and black thigh high boots. She comes to a sudden stop and looks worriedly around the room. "What are you doing!?"

I took a couple of steps back to where I was standing and sighed. "Nothing."

She walked quickly to stood beside me. "Do not lie to me. You were going to try and escape, weren't you?"

Yes.

I rolled my eyes. "Of course, I wasn't."

She shook her head. "You're lying. I can see it in your eyes that you want to leave here."

"I can't stay here. I need to go home." I said.

She smiled gently and rested her hand reassuringly on my shoulder. "You are home. With us."

I scoffed at her words. "This is a prison."

She chuckled. "Possibly, but to some, they have no

home to go back to."

I frowned. "Do you not have parents?"

Her eyes saddened. "I do, but whether they are still alive now is something I do not know."

Her words make me think of how she became captured in the first place.

I cleared my throat. "How did you…"

She raises a single brow. "Become a whore for the Jinyoung's?"

I nod.

She released a heavy exhale. "My parents have had a lot of trouble with money in the past, and they borrowed some money from Li Wei. I said some but it was a lot of money. More than my parents could handle. When the time came to pay the money back, they couldn't. Not even half of the amount they owed. Li Wei and his sons held me and my parents at gunpoint until Kang suggested they take me in as a sort of ransom. Li Wei said that if I were to accept as being part of their organisation he would let my parents live and the money my parents owed would be forgotten. How could I not accept the offer? I did what any daughter would do and accepted."

And to think Kang was the one that saved her and her parents' life? That was pretty hard to fucking believe considering what a vile person he was.

I didn't think he had a caring bone in his body.

"What about you?"

I remember back to the time when my mother and I went to the pier that night and witnessed the horror of seeing the brothers dispose of a body.

"Me? I saw Li Wei's sons throw away a dead body in the shore. I thought they hadn't seen me, but they had."

"What a pity."

I continue. "On that same night, they kidnapped me from my own home."

She looked at me in sorrow.

"And now I'm here, and I'll probably be here forever."

She grabs ahold of my hand and gives it a squeeze.

I looked down at our hands clasped together then up at her. "Help me escape. Let's escape together."

Shuang gasped. "Maggie! Do not say such things."

"But…"

Before I can interject, Shuang releases my hand and hands me something. "You dropped your mask on the way here. Put it on, they are coming. And remember the rules."

"I'll do my best." I say sarcastically as I put on the white mask. I bring it to my eyes and tie the ribbon tightly around my head.

"Please, Maggie!"

I nodded at Shuang as three middle-aged men dressed in suits came in and glanced at the two of us. I notice even one man licking his lips.

Keep fucking walking.

I lower my eyes to the ground as more people soon start to come in and begin chatting and laughing amongst each other.

None of them look bothered about the fact that we were here against our will.

Do they even know what's actually going on? If they did, why are they okay with it? They weren't human. They couldn't be.

I felt a warm, dry hand at my lower back and it made me jolt in surprise.

My whole body tensed when I heard Li Wei's voice in my ear. "You look beautiful. Stunning even. If only your father could see you right now. He would be so proud." He skims his finger up my arm. "Being a whore really suits you."

I tense my jaw and continue staring at the ground, but how I wished that I could beat the crap out of him in front of all these people.

"Do not speak to any of these people. Do that and I'll rip out your tongue. Do you understand?" He warned.

"Yes, sir." I try to speak as politely as possible.

He chuckled. "Good girl. You may raise your head."

At that moment, an elderly looking Chinese man comes to shake Li Wei's hand. They exchange a few words in Chinese when the old man suddenly looks over at me with a look of lust in his eyes.

In your dreams.

"*Tā shì xīn lái de ma*?" **(Is she new?)**

Li Wei smiled brightly and wrapped his arm around my waist. "She is new, *shì*. **(yes)** She is pretty, no?"

In this position, I could totally break his wrist.

Do it, Maggie.

"Yes, very pretty." The man responded.

Li Wei chuckled. "I knew you'd like her."

His old eyes gazed at my breasts. "I must have her, Li Wei. When can she service me?"

His words made me want to throw up in my mouth.

"Not yet, I'm afraid. After some training, perhaps?"

The old man scans my body and licks his lips. "*Shì*,

(Yes) definitely. But I hope it will not take long."

Li Wei chuckled. "In time, my old friend. Come and have a seat, food is about to be served."

The meal begins with Li Wei making a speech about his return which is then followed by a toast and the clinking of glasses. The plates are soon brought out. After that, everyone around the table begins talking again. I look down at the table to where Yuta and Kang are sitting. I noticed they were engrossed in talking to a middle-aged man wearing a tuxedo and a beautiful woman who was wearing a bright red dress.

Looking at the crowd makes me think to myself who exactly are these people and why they've come to a fucking whore house. Were they here looking to have a good time or here simply just to kiss Li Wei's ass? I was voting on the latter.

Unexpectedly, Li Wei takes my hand and pulled me to sit on his lap. I didn't fight him. But I wanted to.

He rests one hand on my knee and reaches for his fork with the other. He taps it gently along his glass and immediately, the room goes silent "Ladies and gentlemen. Before I release you and allow you free reign of my beautiful home and of my beautiful women, I wish to give one of my oldest friends an early birthday gift. As you all know, his birthday is just around the corner and I wish to give him his present now. Therefore, for this night's entertainment,

Shuang here will begin the celebration." Li Wei turns to the old man who wanted me to sit next to him and smiles. "Happy Birthday, my dear friend."

The old man looked from Shuang to me, then back to Shuang again. "My friend, I appreciate your early gift very much. Shuang here is very beautiful, but I cannot help myself. I am more drawn to this stunning new girl you have brought here this evening. She is unlike anything I've ever seen before. I can't seem to take my eyes off of her."

Oh no, please no.

Li Wei chuckled. "I meant what I said, my friend. I'm afraid Maggie here is off limits for this evening."

The old man nods in understanding. "Of course, no problem, but the moment she is available, I wish to have her first."

"Of course. You'll be the first to have a taste. That I promise." He motioned to Shuang. "Now, go. Enjoy your gift."

When Li Wei slaps Shuang's behind, the guests around the table laugh and clap their hands together in delight. Shuang wastes no time by dropping on to her hands and knees and prowls over to the old man.

The old man slowly pushes his chair back, stands up and approaches Shuang. Ever so quietly, she lies on her back, takes off her panties and shamelessly spreads her legs open. The man drops to the floor and puts his face between her legs.

From my position on Li Wei's lap, I could see everything he's doing to her. Shuang raises her hips from the ground as he tastes her. I look at her face and she looks to be at peace, but when he flips her over on her hands and knees, her eyes open wide. I feel sick to my stomach when I see that the old man is long and hard as he enters her from behind. I looked around the room and felt like throwing up when I saw the guests touching themselves and seeing the lust in their eyes as they watched.

I couldn't take it anymore.

I looked away in disgust only to meet Yuta's eyes. He must have had some idea of what I was thinking because he shook his head. It was odd because looking into his eyes helped distract me with what was currently happening in the room. Looking into his eyes was somehow helping me. How was that even possible?

He mouthed. "Look at me."

I would've continued on looking at Yuta if it wasn't for Kang. I notice that it was the fourth time he's refilled his glass to the brim, and if I looked carefully at him he had this pissed off look on his face. I followed his line of sight to see that he was looking at the old man fucking Shuang with...jealousy? Did he have some beef with the old man? Or was he watching Shuang?

Li Wei squeezed my knee. “Are you watching?”

When I looked back, I saw that the old man was holding Shuang with his hand wrapped around her throat. She looked to be enjoying every single moment.

I grimaced.

This was wrong. This was rape.

“One day, that will be you, Maggie. Serving every single man here, even me.” He purred into my ear.

I rolled my eyes and without meaning to I scoffed. “I don’t fucking think so, you sick fuck.”

In a split second, everything in the room went silent and all eyes were on me.

Even Shuang’s. But her eyes were full of fear.

Li Wei pushes me off of him, resulting in me falling to the ground and getting kicked twice in the stomach. Pain unlike any other begins to occur inside of me.

“Yuta!” Li Wei roars.

I watched as Yuta tensed his jaw and rose from his chair and bowed at his father. “Yes, sir?”

Li Wei spat on the floor. “Take this whore away, and punish her.”

Yuta's face became stoic as he bowed again. "Yes, sir."

"And, Yuta?"

"Yes, father?"

Li Wei growled. "Do not go easy on her."

Yuta bowed. "Yes, sir."

I glared up at Li Wei as Yuta pulled me roughly from the ground and dragged me from the room.

Chapter 4

Maggie

My heart raced, fear pulsating through my veins. Dread gnawed at my insides as I faced the impending unknown. The weight of uncertainty pressed upon me, casing a foreboding shadow over my thoughts. Anxious thoughts swirled, like a temperature brewing in the horizon, and the fear of what lay ahead gripped my every nerve.

"Let me go, Yuta!"

Dragging me by the wrist, he growled. "Be quiet! You brought this on yourself."

Yuta paused for a few seconds outside a door but then sighed as he led me into a dark room. A shiver ran down my spine when my eyes adjusted to the darkness.

Oh no...

It was some kind of sex torture chamber.

My jaw dropped as I dragged my eyes around the room. In the far corner, was a leather padded bench placed to a huge black king-sized bed. There were chains hanging from the walls and the ceilings. A massive cross in the center of the room, a table with ankle and wrist cuffs, with a layout of dildos, vibrators, and whips.

"Whenever you are brought into this room, you stand in the centre with your head bowed until further instruction. Do you understand?"

I nodded. "I understand."

"Good. Now, take your clothes off." He demanded.

My head shot up and without thinking said. "No."

He approached me slowly. "Take. Off. Your. Clothes. Now."

I hugged my arms over my chest and lowered my head. "Please, don't do this."

"You knew what would happen if you crossed the line and you did. For that, you must be punished. Remove your clothes."

God, I wanted to fight back. I wanted to fight back so hard but what would happen if I did? The world was a scary place, but this place was a hell of a lot scarier.

He growled. "If I have to ask you again, I won't be as kind."

Defeated, I thrusted my chin upwards and with a hateful glare pointed towards Yuta, I unzipped my corset and tossed it aside. He then turned me around and bent me over the edge of the bed. "Don't move."

"Don't hurt me." I whispered. "Please."

He moved away for a few seconds but returned with something in his hands. My whole body tensed as he slipped a blindfold over my eyes.

"You thought you had it bad in America?" Yuta growled in my ear. "You haven't seen anything yet."

I breathed. "Yuta, don..."

A hard smack landed on one of my ass cheeks.

I gasped at the sting.

Fuck!

He spread my legs apart. "You disappointed father tonight. Therefore, you disappointed me."

Another hard smack landed on my ass.

I bit my lip and whimpered.

From behind me, I could hear the clink of a belt being unbuckled and pulled from the loops around Yuta's waist.

My breathing increased instantly. Five seconds later, a vicious sting was followed by another loud whack against my ass. I cry out from the excruciating pain from the belt.

"Stop it!" I pleaded.

Another blow landed before I could even process what

had just occurred.

"Please, stop!" I wailed.

Thwack!

I whimpered with each strike when suddenly I was dragged across Yuta's lap, facedown. He removed the blindfold and reached for something then struck me with it. Whatever he hit me with had me gasping from its intensity. I turned my head over to see a wooden paddle in his hand.

Each strike had me squirming.

I lay there gasping and trembling. My breathing has become so ragged that I could not even speak. My ass was on fire.

"Your punishment hasn't even begun yet." Yuta said as he ran his hand over my ass.

What?

I squirmed as his finger slid down and touched my bundle of nerves. The touch almost sends me through the roof.

"Keep still." He ordered.

He slides a dildo in between my folds, teasing my cunt by sliding it up and down. I moaned, moving my hips with the motion of the dildo. I feel it slide inside of me easily. I felt ashamed because I was so wet. I then felt Yuta part the cheeks of my bottom and slid a large plug into me. The burning from my ass and the plug made my cunt throb. For a second, I swear I could feel my heartbeat in my clit.

"Stand up." Yuta orders.

With unsteady legs, I rose from his lap and stood on my two feet. It takes a sufficient amount of effort. I feel him drawing something up my legs, attaching it to the dildo and the plug inside of me. I was so close, I would have orgasmed if Yuta had kept his finger on my clit. The click of the belt sounded like thunder to my ears. As soon as the lock closed, there was a different sensation. My knees buckled as the dildo began to vibrate inside of me, the plug swelling slightly and vibrating as well. I fall forward into Yuta's arms, thankful for his support as my own body betrays me. I feel the beginning of an orgasm hit me, my muscles clamping down on the dildo. As suddenly as it had begun, the vibrating stopped. I moaned and whimpered, hearing Yuta's laughter in my ear.

"This is a punishment. Not a reward."

He effortlessly picks me up and puts me up against the massive cross. A small yelp escapes my lips when he tightly straps the restraints around my ankles and wrists. I moaned and squirmed as Yuta began flogging me, starting with soft strikes then finishing with more fiercer strikes. He then stops and walks over to a shelf and pulls something out of a drawer. He pulls out a flogger made of long rubber strips, about ten inches in length.

“Stop, please.” I moaned as the first strike kissed my already inflamed skin. I felt myself getting closer and closer, teetering on a cliff.

A tortured moan drags from my throat as the flogging suddenly stops and fire began to slowly trail over her body.

“I can’t take it anymore.” I sobbed.

From all the training I had done in the past, this was by far the worst pain I had ever endured.

Yuta comes to a stop in front of me and cups both of my cheeks. “None of this would’ve happened if you had just behaved, but you had to open your mouth, didn’t you?”

My mouth remained shut.

He shook me and raised his voice. “Didn’t you!? Why can’t you do as you’re fucking told!?”

Up until this point, it was as though what Yuta had been doing this whole time was trying to help me. But this was Yuta we were talking about. He didn't want to help me. He wanted to destroy me.

“I don’t know!” I screamed. "You want me to be this submissive girl who does everything you say, but I can’t be who you want me to be. I can’t!”

Yuta drops his hands from my face. “Can’t or won’t?”

My eyes welled up. “I was raised to be strong. A girl who would fight against evil people like you and your family but because of what you’ve done to me, I’m not the girl I thought I was. You’ve brought me down so much that I don’t think I can get back up.”

“What are you saying?”

“I guess what I’m trying to say is congratulations. You’ve finally got what you wanted from me. Defeat.”

Yuta steps back and puts his hands in his pockets. “You admit defeat? Just like that? You haven’t been here a day and yet you’ve already given up.”

I frowned. “I thought that’s what you wanted?”

He scoffed. “I did, but breaking you now won’t be as fun if you’re already broken.”

“You broke me a long time ago.” I whispered.

He stared at me for a long while, then wrapped his hand around my neck and kissed me. Long and hard. With his lips still on mine, he reaches up and releases my wrists from the restraints. They dropped down and landed on Yuta’s broad shoulders. “I don’t like my women broken. Especially if that woman is you.”

“I’m not yours.” I whispered against his lips. “I’ll never be yours.”

“You were mine the second I laid eyes on you.” He

whispered.

“Then, stop this. All of it. Please.” I pleaded.

“I can't.” He muttered.

“...Why?”

He ignored my question and removed the clasps around my ankles. He pointed to the door. “Your punishment is over. Go straight to your quarters and don’t try to escape. There are guards everywhere and they won't hesitate to shoot you. For once in your life, do as you're told.”

I nodded in understanding as I pushed myself away from the cross, to notice myself wobbling and unable to stand straight from the leftover pain from my abdomen and ass.

As I walked back to my quarters, I felt my heartbeat in the wounds across my lower back, butt, and thighs.

I was so tired.

I headed straight for the bathroom to the nearest shower, the first touch of water against my skin had me flinching and wincing.

I didn’t stay there very long. Drying off was painful. I dreaded seeing what was done to me.

I looked at myself in the mirror to see ugly welts all over my body.

Oh my god.

Without another look, I wrapped the towel around myself, passed the others and headed to my mattress. I passed out as soon as my head hit the surface

Chapter 5
Maggie

I was woken up early the next morning to someone gently caressing my cheek. Without thought, I turn over onto my back only to wince as I remembered the pain that was inflicted on my backside yesterday.

"*Gibun-i eottaeyo*?" **(How are you feeling?)**

I slowly opened my eyes to see Ling sitting on the edge of my mattress, smiling gently at me.

I winced as I sat up. "Sore."

Ling looked at me in compassion. "Shuang told me what happened."

"She did?" I asked.

Ling nodded at my question. "I wanted to check on you to see if you were alright, but when I came to see you last night, you had already passed out."

I recalled the events of yesterday and laid back down on the mattress with a groan, only to wince from the wounds on my body. "After what happened, I wasn't feeling particularly chatty."

Ling nodded again in understanding. "That is understandable. You are new here and receiving a punishment like that must've been a shock."

"I've had worse." I muttered.

"Even so, what made you lash out like that?" Ling asked.

I pictured Li Wei's face and scrunched up my face. "It was just something Li Wei had said. He said something along the lines of, I was going to serve lots of men...repeatedly."

Ling bit her lip. "But he's right. You are a whore."

I raised my voice. "No, I'm not!"

She lowered her head. "But you are. It's what we all are and somehow or another, you're going to have to accept it."

Never.

This wouldn't be how I lived the rest of my life...

"I'm not a whore. I don't care how many times people tell me that I am one, I'm not going to accept it. Ever."

Ling raised her eyes and studied me. "It's true what they're saying about you."

"What are you talking about?" I asked.

"That you're just going to keep fighting; that you're not going to give up until you're free."

There was no hesitation. "No, I won't stop."

Ling reached for my hand and grasped it tightly. “Maggie, do you know how powerful Li Wei is?”

Of course, I did. But my family was also very powerful.

She sighed. “If they have brought you here, that’s it. There is no chance of escape.”

But I will escape.

“Being brought here means that you will be a whore for the rest of your life.” Ling stated.

I pointed at my chest. “Not for me, it won’t. Being a whore was not my idea, and I’m not staying here any longer. There’s a way out of here somewhere and when I do find one, I'm leaving. With or without you.”

She looked at me in pity. “There is no way out.”

I looked around hopelessly. “How do you know that? Has anyone ever tried to escape?”

She shook her head. “No.”

I frowned. “Why?”

Ling shrugged. “Because we’re afraid of the threat.”

My frown deepened. "The threat?”

Ling continued. “When we were brought here, Li Wei threatened to kill our family if we ever tried to escape. Since then nobody has ever tried to run away. We're all scared that the people we love might get hurt if we try to escape."

Yuta told me the exact same thing. But what if they were just words only to scare us, then what?

"Then, what if we try to escape together?" I suggested.

She scoffed. "Did you not listen to a word I just said? They'll kill everyone you love. You're crazy, Maggie if you think you'll get out of here alive because you won't. This family is not to be messed with."

I sat up. "Neither is mine. My father will get us out of here."

I know he will. He had to.

"Who is your father?" Ling asked.

"A very powerful man. Just as powerful as Li Wei."

She looked blankly at me.

"He specializes in finding people and killing them. And I promise you, that he will find us and get us out of here."

She didn't look at all convinced. Instead, Ling lets go of my hand and stood up. "Do not make such promises. We are trapped here. Forever."

Just as I go to speak, Shuang comes into the room with a towel around her body, a peaceful look on her face. "Good morning."

I stood up with the towel around my body and go to

greet her. “Hi.”

Shuang turned to me and reached for my hand. “How are you feeling? Sore?”

I nodded. "Yes.”

She looked at me reassuringly. “Do not worry, my friend. The pain will recede in a few days. You’ll be fine.”

She lets go of my hand and lies down on her mattress.

“Where have you been?” Ling asked.

Shuang yawned. “I was serving four gentlemen. I didn’t think it would go on all night, but they were having so much fun.”

I stuttered. “Four men?”

Shuang nods. “Don’t look so surprised, Maggie. Four is nothing.”

My jaw dropped. “One is enough.”

She smiles shyly. “It’s actually more enjoyable with more people. The men focus on you only, and it makes you feel somewhat special. Maybe someday, you’ll experience it for yourself.”

Was this really going to be my life from now on? Being raped by men day after day? Not a chance.

“Maggie?”

I looked down at Shuang. “Yes?”

“Do you remember that man from last night?”

Which one? There were so many men last night that I didn't have a clue who she could be talking about.

She sees the confused expression on my face and explained. “You know, the old gentlemen who was fucking me?”

Oh god.

What about him?

A shiver ran down my spine. “How could I forget him

“His name is Sal."

Was that name supposed to mean something?

"Do you know who that man is to Li Wei?” Shuang asked.

"I heard that he's Li Wei’s informant. That’s it.” I answered truthfully.

Ling shook her head. “He isn't just his informant. He’s Li Wei’s closest and oldest friend.”

I shrugged. “And I should care, why?”

Shuang sat up, looked over to where the camera was and lowered her voice. “He’s in the villa right now, conversing with Li Wei...and I heard your name.”

My heart stopped.

My name? Why would they be talking about me?

“Why….?” I let the question hang in the air.

Shuang continued. “Li Wei is no doubt upset after what you did last night. You see, he hates upsetting his guests because it ruins his reputation. When you were taken away, Sal did not continue with me. He had left and looked far from happy. And I'm sorry to say this, butLi Wei will want to please him and make amends and because he took such a liking to you, he could make you satisfy Sal.”

My eyes widened in horror. “No! I won't do it!"

Shuang shook her head. “You don't have a choice. You must do as you're told.”

No!

“Hey, new girl!” A voice from the doorway grabbed our attention. We turned our heads to see the girl with the caramel skin with the red bob standing in the archway.

“What is it?” I asked harshly.

"You’ve been summoned. Get dressed and put your face on. You've got your first customer."

She was gone before her words sank in.

"This can't be happening." I looked at the spot where she was just standing when my eyes widened. “Surely not."

"I'll go and pick your outfit for you." Ling lowered her head and exited the room.

I watched her leave and turned to Shuang. "Tell me this isn't happening."

Shuang's face drained of all colours. "I'm sorry."

I whimpered. "No, I can't do it. I'd rather die."

Shuang stood up and placed both hands on my shoulders and shook me. "Listen to me, he may be old but he's kind."

"I don't give a damn!" I spat.

"Four minutes! Can you spare four minutes of your life?"

I scoffed as I headed to my mattress. "No."

A hand grabbed my wrist and pulled me out of the room. I turned around to see Ling pulling me into the dressing room.

"No!" I dug my heels into the ground. "I'm not getting dressed! I'm not doing it!"

Ignoring my words, she hands me a black leather zipper front bustier corset and black heels. "Put them on."

I look at the getup then throw them on the floor. "I said I'm not doing it."

"Maggie, you must do this. It is an order. Do you

really want to be punished again?"

No, but...

Ling grabs the clothes and shoes from the floor and hands them to me. "Come on, get dressed. I'll do your hair."

With much consideration, I take the clothes and shoes from her and get dressed without a word. Ling straightens my hair and does my makeup for me.

Why am I being made to look pretty for him?

I look at myself in the mirror as she applies the last touches of my mascara. "If I asked you for a favour, would you do it?"

"That depends on what it is you're asking for."

A pause.

"Can you make me look...undesirable?"

She chuckled. "Would you like me to?"

I nodded. "Yes."

"Why?"

I shrugged. "Maybe if I looked like undesirable, he might send me back."

Her smile dropped. "I can't do that unfortunately."

"Why?" I asked.

“If I make you look undesirable, I will be in trouble.”

I frown. “Why would you be in trouble?”

“I do all the girls’ makeup. I’m in charge of making the girls look pretty.”

“Why?”

“Before coming here, I was training to become a beauty therapist.”

“What happened?” I asked.

She waved around her. “This happened.”

I didn’t follow.

“I was in college and had a part-time job as a stripper. Back then, I was poor and being a stripper really paid well. I didn't really have a choice but to work there. So, one night, one of the Jinyoung brothers came in and offered me a lot of money to join this organization, and I said yes.”

“Just like that?” My eyes widened. “You said yes to being a whore?”

Ling laughs. “Unfortunately, Chen didn’t mention the whore part. All he said was for me to put makeup on the girls and I would get paid greatly for it, but he didn’t specify what kind of girls they were or the fact that I'd also be a whore.”

What?

I gasped. “Wait? It was Chen!?”

She frowned. “Well, yes. Which brother did you think I was talking about?”

Definitely not Chen.

“Kang?”

She smiles. “Kang is not interested in me. Never has been. I'm not his type.”

“No?”

She shakes her head. “Shuang is the one he desires the most out of the girls.”

“Really? What is their story?” I asked.

“I don't know. All I know is that Kang and Shuang have a lot of history.”

History?

“What kind of history?” I asked.

“Well, aren’t you nosy?” A deep voice said from behind us.

I looked in the mirror to see Kang leaning against the wall just inside the room with an amused look on his face.

Ling stands and lowers her head. “Apologies, sir. We did not mean to offend you.”

Kang leans away from the wall and cups her cheek.

"But you did. Don't worry, you can make it up to me later."

Ling bows. "Yes, sir."

He lets go of Ling and grabs my arm, pulling me out of my seat. "You. Come with me."

With my free hand, I try to remove his tight hold on me. "Let me go."

He of course ignored me and continued on pulling me.

"Kang!"

"Shut your mouth." He barked.

He takes me out of the room and leads me down a narrow hallway. He stops in front of a door and knocks on it.

"Come in." A masculine voice says from inside.

Kang opens the door, leading me into a big, beautiful bedroom. My eyes immediately go to the four poster bed placed in the middle of the room with the old man inside it.

"Wow, what a beautiful sight you are." He groaned.

I closed my eyes and took a deep breath.

Four minutes. That's all. I can do this. I could spare four minutes.

"How are you this morning, Sal?" Kang asked

politely.

Sal pointed at me. “Better now that this woman is here.”

I open my eyes to see Kang standing in front of me. “This man…”

I rolled my eyes. "Is a close friend of your father’s, yes, I know."

Kang backhands me. “Don’t be a fucking smart ass. He’s an important man, so don’t disappoint him. Rule number one, never tell a customer no and rule number two, you will allow him to do whatever he wishes. Break any of these rules and guess what? You’ll be punished.” He leans into my ear. “And try to enjoy yourself even if you don’t otherwise you'll be keeping me company tonight.”

“In your dreams.” I whispered.

He smiles. “Now, Sal might be old but from what I heard, he used to be a stallion back in the day.”

I look away and grimace.

Kang steps back, bows to the old man and leaves.

“Come closer, dear. I won't bite.”

I take a couple of steps towards him and look around the room for any sign of cameras, but none are to be seen.

At this moment, my nerves were on high alert.

This was my chance to escape. With no cameras around, I can surely find a way out of here. If I don't take this chance, I'll regret it for the rest of my life.

"Do not be afraid." Sal said calmly.

My eyes dart around the room and notice a vase standing on the floor next to the window.

"Before we begin, I must use the bathroom. I will return shortly." He gets out of the bed and heads towards the bathroom with a smile.

I watch him leave and grab the vase on the floor. With the vase in my hand, I stand behind the door and wait for Sal to come out. After what feels like hours, I hear the toilet flush and footsteps. I slowly lift the vase over my head, hold my breath as Sal exits the bathroom and when he passes me, I grip the vase over my head and bring it down hard on to his head. The moment the dish makes contact he falls effortlessly to the ground.

Out cold.

I stare at his lying form in disgust and spit. "*Dwaeji.*" **(Pig)**

The whole lot of them were pigs.

I back away from him while wondering what will happen to me now once they find out what I've done. Whatever that may be, I don't want to find out.

So, I climb out of his window and get the fuck out of there. Now, I don't know where my path will lead me, but I refuse to spend another night in this place, locked up in a room, waiting to be used repeatedly.

I will not allow Yuta to ever hurt me again as he did last night. Never again will he see me or lay a hand on me ever again.

****

After months of training and hours spent exercising, I've managed to keep in good shape throughout the years. I'm glad to think that all of the blood sweat and tears I've put in while training hasn't gone to waste.

I run as fast as I can, away from that hell hole and the people inside it. I won't miss Li Wei and his sons one bit, but the girls? I'll miss them the most even though they're completely brainwashed.

I run until the villa is out of view and only then do I slow my pace. I walk for about fifteen minutes and come across a beach. Only when my feet come across sand and rocks that I notice I'm barefoot.

I knew without looking that there were cuts on my feet from twigs and gravel I ran through just to get away, but it didn't matter. This kind of pain, I could take. Not the one in that place. That place they called Paradise. Having to endure that place was the hardest thing I've ever had to do.

After a few more minutes, I come across an old, abandoned shack. Without thinking too much, I run over to it, push open the door and peek inside. To my luck, it was empty.

Cold, but empty. I could sleep here tonight.

I look behind me just to double check that I was not being followed, then enter the small shack and close the door behind me.

I should be safe here for now.

With quivering legs from the exertion, I take a seat on the dirty wooden floors and check my feet. Both feet were slashed but weren't cut deep enough to worry about.

A cut to the foot is nothing compared to what happened to me while being in the hands of the Jinyoung brothers.

Nothing.

As darkness began to fall, I lowered my back to the floor, my arms wrapped tightly around my middle and closed my eyes.

Chapter 6

Yuta

“WHERE. IS. SHE!?” I roared as I pinned my brother against the wall by his throat.

Rage surged through my veins like an unrelenting storm, each heartbeat echoing the intensity of my anger. I was livid. The angriest I’d ever been.

"*Nǚhái zài nǎlǐ*?” **(Where is the girl?)**

Frustration knotted my muscles, and fiery emotions threatened to spill over. But my anger wasn’t pointed towards the girl. It was pointed towards Kang for allowing something like this to happen because if it didn’t involve sex or drugs, he didn’t want to know.

“If I have to repeat myself one more time, I will kill you.”

The world blurred through a lens of red, and every second of silence that passed felt like a searing arrow piercing through the air. The weight of resentment bore down on me, a tempest of emotions that demanded release, leaving me grappling with the turbulent sea of my own wrath.

“*Huídá wǒ*!" **(Answer me!)**

Kang winced as he answered. “Fa…father ordered me to take her to Sal.”

“And do what!?” I ordered, glaring down at him.

I had searched every square inch of the villa, but there was no sign of her anywhere. A gut feeling told me that she was long gone, and the thought of not seeing her again stirred something strange inside of me.

“What did he order her to do!?” I growled.

He stared blankly at me, all the while biting his lip.

I leaned into his face and tightened my grip around his throat. “Tell me, Kang.”

Kang looked around anxiously and whispered. “Because of her behaviour two nights ago, father sent the girl to his old friend...as a way to make amends.”

I was speechless.

I shook my head in distaste and released him. “You left her alone with that frail insect?” I spat.

“I had orders.” He uttered under his breath. “What was I supposed to do? Disobey?” He scoffed.

I snapped in reply. “She could snap Sal like a twig. Or have you forgotten what she’s capable of?”

Kang dropped his head and released a heavy exhale. “Father wanted…”

I cut him off. “I don’t give a fuck what father wanted!

You get her back right now."

Kang's head shoots up so fast he had to take a moment to regain focus. "How!? She could be miles away from here!?"

"Then you better start looking." I replied.

"It's the middle of the night!" Kang snapped angrily.

I screwed up my mouth into a dry smile."I couldn't give two fucks. You lost her, now you find her. Fail to do so, and I will make you pay."

"Brother..." He whispered in distress.

I waved off his pathetic attempt at making me feel remorseful towards him. "Don't come back until you've got her. Do you understand?"

He glared at me but nodded nonetheless. "*Shì* de." **(Yes)**

Chapter 7

Maggie

I was awoken the next morning with a throbbing pain in my left cheek. It felt like something had struck me, and just when I thought that I was probably dreaming, it happened again.

“Ouch...” I groaned in agony at the sudden blow.

Half asleep, I reached up to touch my cheek only for my hands to be shoved away roughly.

“Wake up.” A voice roughly ordered.

I couldn’t make out the voice due to the fact that I was still completely out of it. Therefore I found myself unable to do what was asked of me, and let sleep overtake me until a swift kick to my back sprung my eyes to shoot open.“I said, wake up!”

As my eyes focused on the figure above me, I felt the colour immediately drain from my face because looking down at me with a look of achievement, was Kang.

I whimpered.

He had found me.

A smirk played on his lips. “Well, well, well, what do

we have here?"

When I try to get off from the floor and prepare to defend myself, Kang brings up his foot and placed it on my chest. "Don't fucking move, whore."

"Get off me." I snarled.

He brings up a finger and slowly moved it side to side. "Not a chance. I let you out of my sight once, I won't be making that mistake again."

I peered up at him. "How did you find me?"

He brings his hand down and grabbed a fistful of my hair. "It was easy. You're not subtle at all."

I could only look at him in disdain.

"There were footprints in the sand, and I followed the trail and it led me here. If it wasn't for your blue hair, you would've had me fooled." He added.

For the first time since dyeing my hair blue, I hated the fact of how bright it was. Maybe if it was my original colour, I wouldn't have been found...

If only.

My heart was beating erratically inside my chest, but I wouldn't show him that I was scared about what he would do to me after what I had done. I had attacked Li Wei's oldest and dearest friend and ran away. No doubt, I would be in a lot of trouble for my actions. Another words, I fucked up.Big time.

“What are you going to do to me?” I whispered.

He tilted his head to the side and tutted. “Nothing will happen to you, but your parents will face the consequences.”

My heart pounded. “My parents?”

Kang pulled me up to stand and gripped my shoulders tightly. “You ran away and for that, your parents will suffer for what you’ve done. Surely, Yuta told you that.”

He had. But he’d never find them. They were smart people and handled people like the Jinyoung’s on a daily basis. My father was untouchable and so was my mother. Every time my father left for a job, an army of heavily armed guards came to protect my mother. I didn’t worry about her safety because I knew she was in safe hands.

I looked up at him with a smug look on my face. “Good luck trying to find my father and reach my mother. You won’t be able to get your hands on either of them. You don’t have a chance in hell.”

He lifted a brow. “I don’t?”

I shook my head.

“Well, I hate to break it to you, but we’ve already got your mother.”

My heart stopped.

"...What?" I murmured.

He merely grinned.

"You're lying." I muttered.

He sighed. "As soon as you escaped from Sal's room, our father gave out an order to capture your beloved parents. Unfortunately, we still can't find your father, so we'll just have to torture your mother instead. Thinking about it, maybe doing that might help us capture your father."

I try to remove his foot off my chest, but he pressed down harder. "Are you deaf? I said don't fucking move."

"You leave my mother alone, you fucking hear me!?" I yelled at the top of my lungs. "You even so much as touch a single hair on her head, I'll fuck you up!"

My words receive a slap to the face. "I'll do whatever I damn well please. I'll beat her, kick her, rape her and torture her and there'd be nothing you could do about it. Nothing."

"Please, don't." I pleaded. "She's my mother. She's done nothing wrong. I'll take the punishment for my actions. All of it. Just leave her alone. Please."

He pouted mockingly at me. "I'd love to punish you, but that's not how this works. Maybe you should've thought of that before deciding to run away."

“Kang!” I shrieked.

“Be quiet and get the fuck up!” He pulled me up off the floor by my arm and dragged me out of the shack. “And don’t try anything either. I’m not in the fucking mood to chase you.”

I obediently followed him out of the shack and back towards the villa. It takes us ten minutes to get back to the property, due to Kang speed walking all the way.

As soon as we got inside, the atmosphere in the air was so tense you could cut it with a knife. Every step I took, I could feel the workers watching my every move. I caught the eye of one worker who stopped dusting as she saw me. She looked at me with an expressionless look on her face. I dug my heels into the floor and frowned at her. She looked at me in pity, lowered her eyes then continued dusting.

“What was that all about?” I asked myself.

A sharp tug on my arm brought me back to reality. “You’re the first whore to ever escape this place. They’re wondering what will happen to you. Wondering if this is the last time they ever see you.”

“They should worry about themselves.” I muttered under my breath. "They're just as vulnerable."

He turned to face me and looked as though he might scold me, but the same female worker who looked at me in pity approached us with something in her hands.

On closer inspection, I see that it's a mobile phone.

She handed it to Kang with a bow and skittered away.

Kang help the phone up to his face while wearing a shit-eating grin on his face. I wondered to myself what it is he's seen that's made him smile. I soon find out what it is that's perked him up.

He turned the screen towards me and what I see causes a scream rip from me - It was my mother bound and gagged. My screams quickly get muffled by a hand from someone standing behind me, and on instinct, I grabbed the hand that was on my mouth, swirled around and brought the hand in my grasp onto the perpetrator's back. I immediately know it's Yuta because of his stature and the noise he made when he grunted.

"You're going to wish you hadn't done that." Yuta barked.

I pushed his hand upward which caused him to loudly grunt. "What are you going to do? Because right now, in your position you can't do shit."

He makes a move, but another pull from me has him stopping immediately. "Don't fucking move." I growled.

"Or what?" He grunted.

I leaned into his ear. "I'll break your arm."

“You wouldn’t dare.” Yuta replied.

I widened my eyes. “Don’t test me."

Kang makes a move towards me, but one glare towards him and he stopped. “Move again and your brother’s arm is going to end up in a sling.”

Kang shrugged. “Do it. He’s suffered a lot worse than a broken arm before.”

His words cause me to frown, wondering what it was that Yuta had suffered from in the past, but the distraction causes Yuta to suddenly bend over, making me topple over his back and land hard on the floor. Yuta then grabbed me, lifted me by the arms and placed me onto his shoulder, despite the fact I was doing everything I could to attack him back. But it was no use.

With me over his shoulder, he led me through the villa with Kang following close on his heels.

“*Nǐ zěnme zhǎodào tā de*?” **(How did you find her?)** Yuta asked.

I looked over at Kang to see a satisfied smirk plastered on his face. “Footprints led me to that old abandoned shack, and I found her inside.”

Yuta let out a chuckle. “That shithole of a place is still standing?”

“Barely.” Kang answered.

I hear a door creak open and the smell of damp air and sweat invades my senses. “Well done for finding her, brother.”

"It wasn't like I had a choice." Kang uttered.

Yuta chuckled.

I didn’t know where they were taking me. Wherever it was, I knew I wasn’t going to like it. I make another fighting move, but I’m dropped to the floor like a sack of potatoes. I get up from the floor only to hear the door slam shut. I felt like a wild animal as I ran to the room. I kicked it, slammed it, clawed at the door hoping it would somehow open, but it didn’t budge. My whole body was thrumming and by the time I dropped to the ground and cried.

I cried like never before and prayed over and over.

“Please tell me she’s okay. Please tell me she’s alive.” I begged, pleaded to the Gods that she was alright, but after what I had seen on Kang’s phone, she was far from alright.

I crawled to the door and pressed my ear against it.

Silence.

“Yuta!?” I banged the door with an open palm. “Kang!? Anybody!?”

Again. Silence. I was alone.

I took a seat on the floor and closed my eyes. I sat on

the cold, damp floor and listened. The only thing I could hear was my own heart beating rapidly inside my aching chest.

Nothing else.

I place my hand on top of my heart and lower my head. The picture of my mother, tied up, bound and gagged, looking as though she'd been beaten within an inch of her life was the only thing on my mind until finally, sheer exhaustion took over me.

I whimpered. "*Eomma…*" **(Mother)**

Chapter 8

Maggie

I was lying on the freezing cold floor, facing away from the door when I heard it slowly creak open. I didn't care who it was or what they wanted. All I wanted to know was if my mother was alright. More importantly, alive.

Without moving or looking behind me, I ask. “Is she alive? Tell me that at least.”

“I see you've calmed down a bit.”

The beat of my heart increased at the sound of Yuta's deep and guttural voice coming from behind me.

Ignoring his sarcasm, I closed my eyes and sniffled. “Is she was alive goddammit!"

I heard him sigh behind me. “Don't use the Lord's name in vain.”

“Fuck you and just answer me.” I demanded as I turned to look at him.

His voice hardened. “For the time being, yes. She's alive."

I cried out, relieved that she was alive. If she had died, I never would've been able to forgive myself.

Yuta raised a brow. "But that might change considering what you did yesterday."

I rose from the floor and approached him. "I know it was stupid, but anybody would've done the same thing if they were in my position. I had a chance and I took it."

"*Zìsī de nǚhái.*" **(Selfish girl)** Yuta says while rolling his eyes.

I scoffed. "How am I selfish?"

Yuta's eyes locked onto mine and frowned. "You understood that?"

I do not answer him.

His frown deepened. "I thought you didn't know a lot of Chinese. Why did you lie to me?"

I took a step back and swallowed. Hard.

"Answer me, Maggie!" He ordered.

"You have your secrets and I have mine." I spat.

He reached forward and cupped my bruised cheek - caused by his brother. "And I intend to know each and every one of them, especially the things that give you pleasure."

I slapped his hand away and squinted my eyes. "Good luck."

He scoffed and shook his head. "You're unbelievable,

you know that?"

"Is that a compliment?" I asked, surprised.

"Far from it."

I shrugged. "I never said I was perfect."

He thrusts his finger in my face. "You're fucked up is what you are."

"That makes the two of us."

I will not deny his words because they were true. But I wasn't the only fucked up person in this room.

"Why did you run away when you knew your parents would suffer?" He tilted his head. "Unless you wanted them to suffer."

"Of course, I didn't! My parents are the only people in the world I'd do anything for. I just didn't think they'd get caught. I obviously underestimated your family and your organization."

His gaze darkens. "Indeed, you did."

A pause.

"Will you… set her free?" I whispered.

He thinks for a moment while looking at me then nods. "'I'll release her on one condition."

I take a step closer to him. "I'll do anything."

Yuta looks at me with a wicked look in his eyes.

"*Josimhae*. **(Careful)** I haven't said what I want in return from you yet."

I didn't care what he wanted from me.

All I wanted was for my mother to live freely and not be held against her will like I currently was. .

I wave him off. "Whatever it is, I'll agree to it. Just let her go."

He chuckled. "*Nǐ bù zhīdào nǐ zài wèn shénme*." **(You don't know what you're saying)**

My voice rises. "I know exactly what I'm saying. Surely you'd understand if your mother was bound and beaten, you'd do the exact same thing."

Anybody would do the same. If they were human. Which Yuta was not.

Yuta immediately stops laughing and spits on the floor. "My mother was a whore. A whore that opened her legs for anybody, much like yourself."

I glared at him only to have it returned.

"Lowering her body to the ground was the best thing that ever happened to me. Having a whore as a mother was fucking embarrassing." He uttered with disgust.

I studied him.

"You killed her, didn't you?" I gritted out.

"I may as well have." He looked at me numbly.

Monster.

He continued. “But no, I didn't kill her. I stood next to my father and watched her sleeping form as he pulled the trigger. Her blood splattered the two of us in the face… and we laughed. We even had a toast afterward, still soaked in her blood. It was beautiful.”

“What...?" I trailed off.

“You'd think I'd be upset for being motherless, that was if I was normal which I'm not. I miss her but I was so happy when her chest stopped moving. No, I was fucking thrilled.” Yuta began to chuckle. “I replay that night in my dreams, and sometimes I wake up to see my cock hard.”

He wasn't human. He couldn't be.

I grimaced. “You're a sick bastard.”

“Indeed, but now I no longer have to live in shame.”

It was my turn to chuckle. “Even if she's dead, your mother was still a whore. It doesn't matter if she's buried six feet deep in the dirty, cold ground, you're still the son of a whore. Nothing's going to change that.”

He marches towards me and wrapped his hand around my throat. “Remember your place.”

Both of my hands reached up to try and lessen his grip on me, but it was useless. "But it's true, whether you like it or not."

He turned me in his arms, my back to his front and held me firmly against him. "You don't know shit about me."

I knew he was asking for a fight. I knew it was coming as soon as he came down here. If it were any other day, the adrenaline inside my body would be thriving right about now, but I was too weak. It had been hours since I had eaten, I had no energy to fight him, but I'd still try even if it was exhausting to do so.

I bring up my elbow and ram it back into his chest. When I feel his grip loosen, I turn around and swing a punch towards his face, but he sees it coming and blocks it by grasping my wrist. With my arm now in his hold, I bring up my leg and kick him in the gut, making him release me and drop to his knees.

"Are we done?" I asked.

He looks up at me with a smirk, then drives his foot into my knee cap, causing me to fall back on hard ground. Yuta gets to his feet and removes his waistcoat swiftly. "I haven't even started."

I crawled backwards. "Stay away from me."

He threw his waistcoat aside and started unbuttoning his shirt. "Not until I've punished you for what you did yesterday."

“Touch me and I'll break your wrist.”

He continued forward with confidence. “I'm counting on it.”

I wait until he's close and stretch my leg horizontally to make contact with his head, but he jumps away from the kick. As he recovers, I run to him, grab him by his neck and pin him against the wall, using my free fist to collide with his face repeatedly. I'm taken aback when I notice him laughing between every punch.

I frowned and held up my fist in mid-air. “Something funny?”

“*Shì, de nǐ.*” **(Yeah, you)** He says, coughing and spitting blood on the ground.

His eyes met mine. “You looked almost ready to kill me.”

“Don't put any ideas inside my head.”

He frowned. “After everything I've done to you, you've never thought of killing me?"

I lower my hand from his neck and walk to the other side of the room. “I haven't, but someone will. One day, you're going to piss off the wrong person and that'll be it.”

I feel his hand pressing on the small of my back, not only that but also a cold blade touches my skin. “Will that person be you, I wonder?"

"It won't be me because I'm not a murderer unlike you." I spat.

Suddenly, he bites my neck.

At first, it hurt, the pain almost unbearable, but then he began to suck the spot, as though he was giving me a love bite. I flail my fists at his chest, but Yuta catches both of my wrists, twists them and holds them in one of his big hands at the base of my spine.

The spot where he bit throbs with pain even though he isn't touching me any longer. It almost felt as though he was branding me.

He throws me to the ground and straddles me. Frustration and anger boil inside of me when I find myself unable to buck him off of me. He was far too heavy and solid compared to my current weak state.

I watch in apprehension as he takes a knife from his waistcoat. He twirls the knife around in his fingers, then slowly brings it down to my chest.

My chest heaves. "What are you doing?"

Without answering me, he uses the knife and swiftly cuts through the corset I've been wearing for over a day effortlessly and separates the bodice, revealing my firm breast. As soon as his eyes lock onto them he begins heaving like a ravaged beast.

“Maggie?” He asks with a whisper.

I avoid his eyes. “What?”

He grasps my chin roughly and stares intensely into my eyes. “You shouldn't have run from me, and because you did, I'm going to hurt you. I'm going to hurt you so badly.”

My eyes grow wide with fear. “You're going to hurt me?”

He just stared at me.

I knew it was a losing battle.

I was far too weak.

Yuta dives down, his stubble scratches against my soft skin as he touches my breasts. He reaches back up to my neck and bites me again. I writhe against him while trying to fight him off, but he grabs both of my wrists and slams them on the floor above my head. He holds my wrists in one hand, then reaches down to my breasts and pinches my nipple. I bite my tongue to stop myself from moaning out loud, but when he pinches a little harder, a small moan escapes my lips.

“*Ānjìng*.” **(Quiet)** He commanded, squeezing my wrists hard, causing myself to wince from the pain he's inflicting.

I was trying to keep quiet, even bit my own tongue. I hated the fact that I was becoming aroused with what

Yuta was doing to me and my body.

“Is this my punishment?” I breathed, trying to buck him off me as his mouth showered kisses all over my torso.

He presses his solid body against mine and runs his nose along my jaw. “I'm not going to punish you tonight. No, I'm going to show you how hurt I was when I found out you ran away from me.”

“Yut...” I breathed.

He cuts me off. “Don't move or I'll fuck you.”

I was too tired to move, and even the thought of fighting with him again exhausted me.

No, I wouldn't move.

Not this time.

He pulls his hands away and unzips his trousers. I watch him as he pulls his leather-clad belt from the loops and encircles the belt around my wrists tightly together. He pulls himself out of his trousers and I gasp to see that he was already hard.

Without a word, he grabs a fistful of my hair and pulls me towards his long, thick length.

I bring myself to my knees and scowl up at Yuta.

He raises a brow. “Lick it.”

I shrink back away, but with a tightened grip on my

hair, a jerk to my head, the tip of my tongue somehow finds itself at the tip of cock.

This wasn't me. I wasn't a whore. Far from it.

Before Yuta, I had only slept with one person, and that was when I lost my virginity. Since that horrendous experience, I tended to stay away from boys. Well, back then I didn't have time for boys.

I only ever had time to train.

I recoil away from him, but he strikes my cheek.

"Suck it." He snarled.

I point a hateful glare in his direction. I hated that fucking word so much, and he knew it too. I knew without a doubt that he kept saying it to get me, but it was fucking working. These days, he seemed to know exactly how to push my buttons.

I didn't like it one fucking bit.

"Do as you're fucking told." He places his hand at the back of the head and leads it at the pace he wants. He fucks my face with no concern for my comfort. No, he just continues on shoving himself to the back of my throat.

I peek at him to see his head thrust back in pleasure, his mouth closed. Raspy groans escaped from the back of his throat as he continued plunging deeper into my throat.

I pulled away, fear that I would choke when his dark, soulless eyes met mine. “What’s the matter?”

I don’t say anything.

He tilted his head and smirked. “What? You don't like getting your face fucked?”

I spat on the ground and wiped my mouth.

He chuckles to himself then lowers onto his haunches, meeting me eye to eye. “Get used to it. After feeling your lips around my cock the first time, I knew once wouldn’t be enough with you.”

He placed both of his hands on my inner thighs and pushed them apart. I wanted to resist and start another fight, but it was hopeless. If I gave him what he wanted now, perhaps he might leave me alone for a while. I allow him to push me onto my back, and as my eyes settle upon the ceiling, I feel his tongue slide inside of me. A loud moan escapes me as my legs try to wrap themselves around him, but he clamps down on my inner thighs with his fingers.

Yuta runs his tongue up my entire opening, lapping up the juices that leave my body.

“Fuck...” He groaned.

I close my eyes and wonder how long all of this would take.

He sucked on my clit, and with my hands still bound

by his belt, I reached down to him and ran my hands through his hair when an explosion of relief erupts from my clit.

I gasp as little pulses of electric warmth rolled away from my core like a shattering earthquake.

He pulls away and brings me up to my knees. I fall forward into his solid chest. “Tired?”

I couldn't bring myself to respond.

“I asked you a question.” Yuta said softly.

My neck is pulled back by a firm tug on my hair. “I don't like repeating myself, Maggie.”

I gaze dazedly up at him and nod. “*Ne, pigon haeyo.*” **(Yeah, I'm tired)**

“That's too bad because we're far from finished.”

He switched me over onto my front and roughly pulled my hips back towards him. His swollen shaft rubs up and down my already wet slit. I bite my lips and scrunched up my face from the guilt of being aroused by his teasing. He runs his fingers up and down my mound, leans over on top of me and wraps a hand around my throat. He whispers in my ear all sorts of filthy, horrible words while running his nose along the side of my head. My body purrs at all the names he calls me, leaving me feeling astounded.

What was wrong with me?

How had it all come to this?

I despised this man, that much was true, but my own body was betraying me. Again.

I whimper when I feel the warmth of his head resting against the lips of my pussy. I feel the muscles of my inner walls clench, waiting to be filled.

Yuta releases my throat and grabs a fistful of my hair. "Do you want me?"

I grunted. "No."

With his hand, he reaches down and cups my pussy. He chuckles and pulls my hair. "You're lying to me."

"*Ani, nan aniya.*" **(No, I'm not)**

His stubble rubs against my cheek as his lips caress the curve of my ear. "If you want my cock inside of you, beg for it."

He was taunting me.

"Beg for it, Maggie." He says in a low, gritty tone.

No.

He slips his head inside of me but pulls away at the last second. "I said, beg me."

I closed my eyes and took a deep breath. I had two options. I could continue giving him the silent treatment, or give him what he wanted and get this over and done with.

I chose the latter.

“Please.” I whisper.

“I can't hear you.” He strikes my behind.

Thwack!

“Please.” I say louder.

“I still can't hear you.” Yuta says cruelly and smacks my behind again.

Thwack!

“Please.” I say a little louder than before.

I gasp when he slowly slips his cock inside of me but then he stops.

“Louder, Maggie!”

If I didn't give him what he wanted, this would never end.

“Fuck me.” I say firmly while glaring at the wall in front of me.

With a satisfied groan, Yuta pushes his entire length inside of me. “Good girl.”

I cry out while reaching with my bound hands to touch the wall to steady myself. His length curves into me slowly, deeply and painfully.

“Say that again, Maggie.” He pulls himself out of me and impales me again.

“Fuck me.” I whimpered, my voice laced with shame.

He thrusts violently inside of me, repeatedly.

The louder I moaned, the harder he fucked me.

The jail type room's silence was filled with the sounds of Yuta's hips slapping the soft flesh of my ass. He places his arm under my stomach and continues to pump into me, stroking me deeply making me moan low in my throat. I closed my eyes, as I felt his solid chest press down on my back. He rocks into me, the closeness of his position makes the feeling of our connection almost intimate. My eyes shoot open as my core begins to pulse.

“You're going to come on my cock?” He asks.

I nodded my head rapidly.

“Come for me.” He whispers as his hand reaches down and rubs my mound, giving the right amount of pressure to my overstimulated clit.

Gripping his cock, I pulse around him and gasped. “Oh my god.”

Yuta's thrusts pick up and become harder. He lifts himself off my back and grabs my hips tightly, pulling me back into his thrusts. All I could do was moan and whimper as he continued fucking me.

Yuta keeps his pace until a growl escapes him and his warmth shoots inside of me. Without a word, he pulls out of me, undoes the belt around my hands, changes, then leaves.

As soon as he closes the door behind him, he peers at me through the steel bars. “Oh, and the promise we were talking about?”

I frowned. “What promise?”

He tutted. “The promise you agreed to, for me to leave your mother alone.”

Recognition filtered in. “What is it? This promise.”

He grinned. “You are to never leave this place, understand?”

“That's it?” I asked.

He lowers his head and shakes his head. “I might've let you off easy this time, but it won't happen again.” He looks at me with a malicious look in his eyes. “You ever dare try to escape this place again, I'll put a bullet between your mother's eyes. Could you live with that?”

I run to the door and scream through the bars. “Fuck you! Fuck the whole lot of you!”

He turned around and leaves. “Eat your soup.”

Without another word, Yuta leaves.

I swirl around to see the bowl of soup on the floor. He must've put it there when he came in. Nevertheless, I won't eat it. I didn't have the stomach to eat it. Without thinking, I kick the bowl of soup against the wall and watch in anger as the food splatters everywhere.

What was I going to do?

Alone again, I look down at my hands to see them trembling.

“What have I done?” I mutter to myself.

Chapter 9

Maggie

When I wake up the next morning, I was surprised to see myself back in the slave quarters. I noticed Shuang and Ling already awake in their beds, but neither of them say a word to me, only cast nervous glances towards me. I knew what their looks meant. They thought my parents were dead, but they didn't know the truth. That

I gave them both a small smile. "They're not dead."

Ling gasped. "*Mwo*?" **(What?)**

Shang's eyes widened. "They're alive!?"

I nodded as I sat up on the mattress.

"How is that possible?" Shuang asked. "Everyone here knows that if you attempt to escape, they'll kill everyone you love."

Ling nodded in agreement. "That's why none of us have dared to escape. We'd hate it if something happened to our loved ones."

There was a long pause until the next person spoke.

"What happened? When you didn't come back from servicing Sal, we all got worried. Even them." Shuang pointed to the other girls who were sleeping heavily.

I remembered back to the day of the escape and released a heavy exhale. "I didn't serve Sal."

Both girls gasped in horror.

"You didn't!?" Ling asked.

I shook my head. "*Ani*, **(No)** I didn't."

I told them everything what had happened that day. They were fully engrossed with what I had to say and by the time I finished, they said I got off lucky; that not every girl would have been so lucky...whatever the hell that meant. I didn't know what they meant by that. I mean, do they have any idea what I've been through? No. They've got no fucking idea. They knew nothing. Yes, my mother had a second chance but what if Yuta lied just to keep me here.

Guess I'll never know. Nevertheless, I didn't feel very lucky. Not really. Now, I felt more trapped than ever.

"Is anyone hungry?" Ling asked.

Shuang sighed. "All of the cupboards are empty."

"Did they forget to stock up on supplies?"

Ling shrugged. "I don't know."

I frowned. "There's no food?"

Shuang bit her lip and said in a low voice. "They usually confiscate the food when mistakes are made. It's a way of punishing us."

I scoffed and motioned towards the kitchen. "There was enough food in there to feed an entire army."

Ling scoffed. "And they'll throw it out just to teach us a lesson."

Baffled at their words, I ignored the fact that I was naked and made my way to the kitchen. The first place I go to is the refrigerator, and when I open it, I'm surprised to see that it was completely empty. Frowning, I closed the door of the refrigerator and looked inside all of the cupboards. They too were also empty. Everything was gone.

Had they emptied the room of all the food because of me?

Realisation setting in, I looked back at Shuang and Ling to see them both looking at me with blank expressions on their faces.

Were they being punished.....because of me?

****

Hours passed and still nobody came to feed us. After everyone had woken up, each one of us went about our business. While the girls did their own thing - showering, reading, painting nails, I dressed in a white camisole and continued to rest on the mattress and stared into space.

By the time afternoon came around, still, nobody came to give us our lunch, nor had the kitchen been restocked. Never before had I been in such a weak state. I hadn't eaten for two days and barely had the energy to do anything.

I hoped that the girls had been fed in those two days, but I wasn't counting on it. Something inside of me was saying that they hadn't. I knew deep down that they had suffered. They've been starved because of my foolish actions.

"*Jeongmal mianhae.*" I whispered. **(I'm so sorry)**

With an exasperated sigh, I curled myself on the mattress, preparing to rest when the door to our room finally opens. Every single one of the girls, including myself, moved toward the entrance. The last person I expected to see was Li Wei, but here he was, in the flesh. We bowed our heads in greeting, and waited for further instructions. Inside my chest, my heart was pounding. I didn't trust myself around Li Wei, and after what happened with Sal, I didn't think I was in his good books. No, I was fucking far from it.

"Maggie, come with me." He said in a calm and collected voice.

I raised my head from the ground, ignoring Ling’s and Shuang’s worried glances and followed closely behind him. At that point, my stomach grumbles out loud. I hoped that wherever we were going had food and lots of it. I hoped that a fucking buffet was waiting for me, but I knew there wasn’t.

Li Wei was a cunt and I couldn’t forget that.

I followed through the villa behind Li Wei. He leads me to the side of the house where I’d never been. I didn’t even know why this part existed. I noticed there were four armed men guarding the hall.

I frowned to myself.

What the fuck is going on? Where was he taking me?

He eventually stopped in front of a door and I watched as he turned to face me with an expressionless look. “Why did you do it?”

Do what?

He saw the confused look on my face and sighed. “Did you really think I wouldn’t find out?”

I remained silent.

“Did you really think you were going to escape here and succeed?” He mocked.

I didn't hesitate with my answer. “Yes, I did.”

As soon as the words left my mouth, he smacked me

across the face.

He tutted. "You know what kind of man I am and yet you still underestimate me. Since when did you grow balls?"

Had he forgotten who I was? Had he forgotten who my father was? I couldn't help but snicker at his use of words. It was so unlike him considering he was a man of power.

"You dare laugh in my face?" He spat.

I bring my head up and glared. "I'm not afraid of you. Hit me, kick me, fuck me or beat me the hell up, I don't care what you do to me. Just take it out on me and no one else."

"Guess you did grow balls while you were away. It's a shame others have had to suffer because of your selfishness."

"Just leave my parents alone!" I spluttered.

He grinned. "Don't you mean parent?"

My whole entire body freezes. The breath I'd been inhaling had gotten stuck in my lungs. A deep tremble began inside of me, starting from my belly until my hands shook at my sides and my jaw chattered.

"What?" I asked in confusion.

He continued grinning.

My voice rose. “What are you talking about?”

Li Wei backhands me. “Do not raise your voice at me or question my authority.”

I cupped my cheek and whispered. “What have you done?”

“What haven’t I done is what you should be asking me. Because of your little stunt, people who aren’t to blame are getting punished.”

“What do you mean?” I asked.

“Punishing and hurting the people you care about is the only way you’ll learn to not repeat your mistakes.”

For some inexplicable reason, my parents came to mind.

“What have you done?” I repeated. “You’ve done something to them, haven’t you?"

He doesn’t answer me.

“Tell me!” I cried.

He locks eyes with me. “Before you escaped, my snipers were already on standby, and when you attacked my old friend and ran away, I had them killed."

Yuta told me they couldn’t find my father and that he’d let my mother go. Did he lie to me? If so, why did he do it?

“You’re lying.” I say.

Li Wei’s eyes widened. “*Nǐ shuō shénme*?” **(What did you say?)**

“I said that you’re lying.” I say confidently. “Yuta’s told me everything. Stop trying to fool me.”

“Yut...” Li Wei chuckles. “Yuta thinks he knows everything that goes on around here, but he doesn’t. When I heard that he released your mother from our hold, I was furious. Livid. But he’s my son and I’m sure he has his reasons.” Li Wei sighed. “No, your mother is very much alive. After I had the pleasure of beating her almost to death, I wanted to keep her all to myself but my bastard son released her. If I would’ve had my own way, I would’ve been able to fuck you and your mother anytime I wanted or maybe even at the same time. Such a pity.”

Deep down, he was keeping something from me, I just knew it. He wasn’t smirking for anything.

“What have you done!? Just fucking tell me!” I demand.

His voice rises. “Did you honestly think I wasn’t going to do anything about the fact that you’d run away? Unlike some people, I actually live up to my name.”

A pause.

“We found your father. We found "The Bull.”

I shake my head repeatedly. "No."

"Aren't you curious what we've done to him?" Li Wei says in an amused tone.

A burning sensation shoots through my sinuses, especially behind my eyes. My body wanted to cry, but I mustn't show any weakness. Not in front of Li Wei. Especially him.

No, Maggie No tears.

I keep my head down and swallow hard.

"Really? No tears? No remorse? This, I wasn't expecting from you. Oh well, maybe this will help. Come with me." He orders. "I want to show you something."

With my head lowered to the ground, I follow his footsteps when I hear buttons being pressed on a wall panel. A door slid open and Li Wei entered. "Follow."

I follow Li Wei into a high tech room filled with hundreds of screens looking into all different types of rooms. Every corner of the villa was being watched by guards who were heavily armed with guns and earpieces stationed in every corner.

"Nothing escapes me, Maggie. Nothing at all." Li Wei muttered.

I look at the guards on the monitor and close my eyes in embarrassment. At that moment, I wanted the ground to swallow me whole.

"You were watching me the whole time." I murmured while slowly opening my eyes.

Li Wei nodded. "We're always watching."

"You've made me look like a fool." I said

Li Wei scoffed. "You've always been a fool. A pathetic and desperate fool."

I tensed my jaw. "Fuck..."

I'm cut off with a smack across the face. "Finish that sentence and I'll fuck you instead."

I dropped my eyes and held my sore cheek while trying not to throw up in my mouth. I knew I had spoken out of turn, but I couldn't help it.

He puts his finger underneath my chin and pushes my face up until our eyes meet. "Watch this footage with me." He turns my face to a screen and drops his finger.

"*Bòfàng shìpín.*" **(Play video)** Li Wei orders to the man who's sat watching the monitors. The man pushed a button, and a black screen comes to life. It starts off dark, but with more concentration, I focused on one figure and clasped a hand over my mouth to what I saw.

I see a bloodied man with a bag over his head kneeling on the ground. I knew from the man's build and by the clothes he wore that the man with the bag over his head was indeed my father. I just knew by the way he held himself. And his clothes? He always wore the same thing. A black t-shirt and cargo trousers. Always. Years ago, he told me that the reason why was because it gave him the look of someone suspicious and dangerous. Back then, I thought he looked ridiculous, but now....now I just want to hold him close to my chest and never let him out of my sight again.

But it was too late.

Li Wei turned the volume up when a door to the empty room opens. The person who enters the room soon reveals himself and as I focused my eyes, my stomach dropped to see that it was Yuta.

"Yut...? Wha...? Why...?" I couldn't finish any of my sentences.

I was a mess.

I looked up at Li Wei to see him smiling wickedly.

"I sent Yuta to wrap up an interrogation for me because I didn't want to miss the look on your face when he executes your precious Daddy." Li Wei says smugly.

"Please." I pleaded.

His eyes widened. "Please? You're begging me now, are you?"

With tears in my eyes, I nodded repeatedly.

He pouts. “It’s too late for that, darling.”

Instinctively, I grab his wrist and place my forehead on the back of his hand. “Please! Please let him go! I’ll do anything. Anything!”

He removes my hand from him, roughly grabs my cheek and turns it towards the screen. “Keep fucking watching otherwise you’ll miss it.”

I don’t want to watch it!

At that moment, I see Yuta reach for something at his side, and when I see him holding a small, silver scalpel, my eyes start to brim with tears.

“No...” I repeat. “Please!”

I watch as Yuta approaches my father and goes to stand behind him. My eyes widen when I see him placing the scalpel against my father’s jugular.

I resist Li Wei’s hand and fall to my knees in front of him. “Please stop this.” I put my hands up in a prayer position. “Please! He’s my father.”

His expression remains impassive. “It’s too late.”

“What?” I whisper.

Li Wei points to the screen. “This footage is from last night.”

I gaped at him.

“Your father’s dead.” Li Wei cheers while turning up

the volume to the maximum. I hear my father shouting obscenities at Yuta, but he pays him no attention. He instead focuses on the camera that's filming this sickening moment and slides the knife across his neck. With no hesitation.

Did Yuta know that I would be watching?

As much as I wanted to look away from the screen, I couldn't. My eyes were completely locked on the screen. I numbly watch the blood run all the way down his front, and when I see his body going limp, I close my eyes and let the tears fall.

He was gone.

This had to be a practical joke, right? They wouldn't do this. Surely, this was just a joke just to teach me a lesson. It was a mistake. They knew that, right?

"Look at me." Li Wei orders.

With my eyes closed, I shake my head repeatedly.

"Do not make me ask you twice." He bellows.

I count to ten, wipe my damp cheeks and slowly peel my eyes open.

"Why the tears? You knew what would happen. You yourself are to blame. You've brought this on yourself."

I stand up and wipe my eyes. "That wasn't him."

Li Wei raised a brow. “No? Are you sure? Because I could show you his head if you wish? You see, I cut off my enemy’s heads as a souvenir. Would you like to see your fathers head?”

"It's not him." Tears choked my voice. “You’re only trying to scare me.”

Li Wei’s face changes to anger and wraps his hand around my neck. “Trust me when I say that the man in the footage is indeed your father. As of last night, he’s dead. Gone forever.” He lowers his voice. “You ever make another mistake like running away again, and it’ll be your mother next.”

Eomma!

Before I can register his words, he brings his mouth down and plants a kiss on my lips. He pulls away and cups my cheek. “Your father’s last words were ‘I love you, Maggie.’”

I glared at him.

"Isn’t that sweet?” He asked with a smile.

I’ll kill him. I’ll fucking kill them all.

Li Wei chuckles as he releases me and taps the guard sitting by the monitors to stand. “*Dài tā zǒu.*” **(Take her away)**

The guard rushes to a stand and bows. “*Shì de xiānshēng.*” **(Yes, sir)**

The guard grabbed my upper arm and without a word led me back to the quarters.

Chapter 10

Maggie

I couldn't wrap my head around what had just happened. My mind was foggy as I was dragged back to the slave quarters. My eyes were burning from all the crying and nothing at all seemed to make any sense. People couldn't be that cruel...could they?

I whimpered. "*Appa...*" **(Father)**

"*Ānjìng de*!" **(Be quiet!)** The guard beside me shouted.

I was too stunned to fight back.

The minute I reached the room, the guard opened the door and shoved me inside, slamming the door behind me. Broken and lost, I swirled around and kicked the door in my temper.

"Maggie?" A soft voice called my name from somewhere in the room, but I ignored it.

Growling, I gripped the door handle and shook it continuously.

"It's locked." One of the girls uttered sarcastically.

Somebody gently placed their hands on my shoulders, but I wasn't in the mood. Far from it. I didn't want to be comforted. I didn't want to be spoken to. I just wanted to be left alone and release my anger out on something...or somebody.

I slapped whoever the hands belonged to away and collapsed onto one of the dining room chairs. As soon as I was seated, I buried my head in my hands and cried.

"Maggie?" A soft voice asked.

I recognised Ling's voice, but I couldn't bring myself to answer her. I couldn't bring myself to even look at her.

My stomach was all over the place. I didn't know whether it was because I wanted to eat or throw up. My entire body was trembling. Was it because I was in shock or was it anger? Or maybe both?

"Fuck." I whispered, as I ran my hands through my hair in frustration.

"Maggie?" Ling asked again. "*Gwaenchanh-a*?" **(Are you okay?)**

No, I was far from okay.

I took a moment to myself and breathed, before turning around and faced the girls in the room. They were all standing in a semi-circle in the kitchen, staring at me with their eyes weary. I slowly stood, still trying to process my thoughts. It was Shuang that spoke first, her voice low and soft. I lifted my eyes and stared into her chocolate-brown eyes.

"Are you okay? Are you hurt?" She asked.

I scoffed and shook my head. "I'm not okay."

Far from it.

She doesn't bombard me with questions to which I was grateful for. She instead smiled reassuringly at me. I tried to smile back, but it comes out wobbly and broken.

"Where did you go? Did you get punished?" One of the girls asked, tucking her red hair behind her ear.

I avoided her eyes. "I'd rather not talk about it and I'd appreciate it if you all left me alone."

"Magg..." Ling whispered my name.

"Just go." I squeezed my eyes closed. "Please."

I knew that Ling and Shuang would respect my wishes and leave me alone, but the other girls wanted answers. They were the type of people who asked multiple questions and refused to leave you alone until they were satisfied. But I didn't know how much self-control I had left.

"What happened to you?" Another girl asked.

I glared up at her. "I asked you all to leave me alone. Why are you all still here? You deaf?"

The same girl scoffed. "What crawled up your ass?

We're just curious to know where you've been for the last two days."

I clenched my fists and snarled. "It doesn't concern you or anybody else. Leave it at that."

"No. Considering it's your fucking fault we're starving, we have a right to know." The girl with the red hair spat.

That's it.

I shoved myself from the chair and marched towards her until we were nose to nose. "I suggest you mind your own business, you fake ass bitch."

Her jaw dropped. "What did you just call me?"

"I called you a fake ass bitch because it's what you are. You're trash." I uttered.

She gasped and shoved my chest. "What's your problem?"

My whole body grew hot with anger.

Kill.

I shoved her chest. "Right now, you're my problem by not leaving me alone when I asked you nicely."

She squared up to me. "I don't do what I'm usually told by the likes of you."

I shoved her again. "Well, maybe you should fucking start otherwise you'll regret it."

She didn't hesitate with her answer. "No."

I motion to the archway that leads to the bedroom. "Leave before I lose my temper."

She scoffed. "What are you going to do about it if I don't leave?"

I looked up at the camera that was on top of the door, then back at her. "If you don't get out of my face, I'll kill you."

Releasing a shriek, she charges at me. Just in time, I tackled her to the ground as she yelled obscenities in my face. I ignored them and punched her in the face. Her face contorts into a rage, her expression feral. She launches herself forward, taking me by surprise. My ears filled with ringing as she screamed. She grabs handfuls of my hair, yanking as we roll, kicking, kneeing, snarling. I grabbed her wrists to try and subdue her, but she was too strong. I cut into her shoulder and she screeches in pain. I then, bring up my foot and kick her back. Panting, she comes to her knees with blue strands of hair between her fingers.

"Fuck. Off." I warned.

Instead of actually fucking off, she wheeled around and punched me in the face.

Fuck!

I reached up with my fingers and touch my bloodied

lip. I rub the blood against my fingers and chuckle. "Wow, that actually hurt."

She marched up to me, and with a roundhouse kick to the side of her head, she fell to the ground like a sack of potatoes.

I pointed to her still body. "Move and it'll be the last thing you ever do."

No response.

As I turned to leave, strong fingers bit into my upper arm, spinning me around.

My eyes focused immediately onto Yuta's face, and I just saw red. He made a noise in the back of his throat as he glared at me. "What's going on here?"

When I don't respond, his forehead furrows, his expression turning pissed. "When I ask you a question, I expect you to answer it. What's going on and why were you two fighting?"

I spat in his face. "Like you don't know."

He wipes my saliva from his face and gripped my arm tighter. "Do you want another punishment?" He asked, his deep, accented voice stiffened my nipples, even as the thrill of fear jolted through me.

"Fuck you, Yuta!" I raised my hand to slap him, but he catches it mid-air, causing me to stumble backward.

He frowned. "What's gotten into you?"

“Get your hands off me, you murderer.” I gritted out.

His jaw clenched as his fingers bit deeper into my arm. “Murderer?”

All I could think of was: attack. Attack him relentlessly. Kill him. Kill him as he did to my father. He deserved it.

Twisting my arm, I rolled my shoulder to get his hand to drop, but he doesn’t budge. He instead leant closer, his eyes delving deeper into me. His stare made me feel exposed and trapped.

“Why are you calling me a murderer?” Yuta demanded.

“Because you are one!” I spluttered. “You killed my father!”

“So what if I have? What are you going to do about it?”

I clutched my heart and staggered backward.

He admitted it to me.

Why did some part of me hope that he would deny it and tell me that it was somebody else?

He shook me by the shoulders. “What are you going to do about it?”

What could I do? Nothing. Not if I wanted my mother to stay alive.

"Answer me." He growls.

A pause.

"Mag..."

I look up at him. "You lied to me."

He remained silent.

"You lied to me, you bastard!" I shrieked.

Without a word, he dragged me by the arm out of the quarters and down all different corridors inside the villa. He eventually leads me into this massive room. He opens the door, the room, light and open.

The walls were plain. There was not a single picture or painting hanging on the pale blue walls. The white spotless carpet was in perfect condition. There wasn't a single dirty spot to be seen. His bed was plain, with white linens and a light blue duvet. It looked so comfortable that my hands twitched from wanting to touch the material on my fingertips. Every single thing in this room was nice. Nice but simple. I liked it but I was jealous. Jealous of being holed up in a shithole of a room while the criminal's living in luxury.

Yuta shoves me inside and blocks the door. I walk in further and close my eyes in delight as my feet sink into the plush carpet. I look over to the window and I feel a pang of pain rip through my chest. I wanted to escape. I wanted to smell the fresh air every day and feel the wind in my hair, but the chance of that ever happening again is slight.

My mother's life was on the line.

"I'll let you call me a bastard slide. Call me it again and I'll hit you."

I met his eyes. "Why did you kill him?"

He lowered his head. "I did it because I was told to."

"*Nugu*? **(Who?)** Your father?" I spat.

"Not only is he my father, but he's also my *boseu*. **(Boss)** Whatever he tells me to do, I do it. No questions asked."

I scoffed. "So, if he told you to jump off a cliff, you'd do it? Wow, you're such a fucking brown nose."

"Call me whatever you want, but that won't change what I've done." He muttered.

I marched until I'm standing right in front of him. "No, it doesn't. Doesn't change a single thing."

He tilted his head. "What do you want from me?"

I shouldered past him. "I want nothing from you.

Grabbing my wrist, he swirled me back around to face him and searched my eyes. "You want an apology? Is that it?"

I stared in appall and knitted my brows. "It doesn't

matter if you did because you wouldn't mean it."

It makes me wonder how many people he's killed by working for his father. How many families were suffering because of him?

"Do you want me to feel guilty for killing your father?"

I snapped my head around and shrieked. "Yes! What you did was wrong! Killing people is wrong. If you don't think that's wrong..."

He cut me off. "If you hadn't run away in the first place, he'd still be alive."

I rolled my eyes. "Don't give me that bullshit. You've been trying to get ahold of my father for years and now that you've murdered him, you're putting the blame on me just to make me feel bad."

He thrusted his finger into my face. "*Dangsin-eun geuga jug-eun iyuibnida*!" **(You're the reason he died)**

I growled out my frustration. "You killed him! You're the murderer here! Not me!"

Yuta's voice rose. "I know what I am and I don't need someone like you pointing that fact out."

I trailed my eyes up and down his body and snarled. "Someone like me? Do you even know who I am?"

He looked down at me in boredom. "I don't care who

you are. I only think of you as a whore. My whore."

I grimaced at the lone word.

Not wanting to spend another minute in a room with my father's murderer, I ask him the reason why he's brought me here. "Why am I here? Are you going to punish me? Fuck me? Or did you bring me here so that you can slit my throat too?"

He showed his annoyance by rolling his eyes and sighing. "I brought you here to get yourself cleaned up. You haven't bathed in over forty-eight hours and it's starting to show. You stink."

Before I can think of a come-back, he grabs my upper arm and leads me to the ensuite. I step further inside and stare into the large bathroom. Inside, there's a large tub, a large glass showers, and a double glass vanity sink. My eyes settle on the mirror, and for some reason, I have this sudden urge to look at myself. I wanted to see what this horrible place had done to me.

"Give me some privacy." I curled my fingers around the basin and look up.

I'm surprised to hear the door to the bathroom close seconds after my promise. Some part of me thought he'd stand and watch me while I was washing. Maybe deep down, he actually felt guilty.

Who was I kidding? He's Yuta fucking Jinyoung. He doesn't give a shit.

I lifted my head up slowly and stare into the mirror. A pair of empty and hollow eyes look back at me. My exhaustion shows as huge black circles surround my green eyes. I didn't recognize the girl looking back at me. My hair had grown past my shoulders but looked like a bird's nest. Where in the past, I had curves some girls would die for, now I looked like a frail looking thing that could break any bone if touched.

I recoiled from my reflection and took off my clothes. I swing the shower door open and walk inside, turning the faucet on. Hot warm comes pouring out, cascading over my skin. I leaned down, picked up the bar of soap and ran it all over my body. Although it's nice to shower without any of the girls around, I don't want Yuta to think that I'm taking my time to shower just to stay in his company. The only reason why I didn't argue with him was that I did actually stink.

The water cascaded down my hair and all over my body. A slight breeze tickled my nipples and they responded with hardened tips. The shower curtain opens. Yuta's unexpected entry didn't surprise me. I knew he'd come. He didn't trust me. He didn't have to say a word. I could feel his eyes watching me as I showered. I closed my eyes and rinsed off the shampoo, along with all the stress and misery of today.

I was…heartbroken.

I opened my eyes just in time to see him step into the

shower fully clothed. His white shirt immediately gets drenched by the water. He picked me up effortlessly and placed me against the shower wall, hugging me tenderly. I stared into nothingness, until Yuta kissed me. What started as an innocent peck, turned into instant hunger. Mouths tightening, tongues twining.

Yuta's arms gripped around me tighter, as he pressed me even harder against the wall. My arms instinctively wrapped around his neck and our lips melted into one. He sucks on my bottom lip and a small moan escapes from my lips. I could feel him hardening between my parted legs. One of his hands wrapped tightly in my blue hair while the other squeezed my ass. He moved his tongue in and out of my mouth, used his teeth, and held me while he ate me up and sucked me in.

"Yuta…" My voice was a whisper.

He lowered me gently to the floor. His eyes were heavy-lidded. "I'm not sorry, but seeing you like this…makes me want to be."

I pushed him away and shot him a wide-eyed stare. He grabbed a towel and wrapped it around me and slowly dried me off. I stared into his face, it was completely blank. "Why did you do it? And please don't tell me it was because you had to."

I wanted to know the real reason why. Desperately. I didn't want any bullshit. Just the simple truth.

"Would you have preferred it if my father killed him? Isn't it better for him to be killed by someone you despise?" Yuta asked.

I scowled at him. "I didn't hate you that much before, but now because of what you've done, I've never wanted to kill someone so badly."

He stayed quiet for a moment then whispered. "I don't blame you."

Chapter 11

Chen

Life...was rarely fair.

As humans, we all make mistakes and naturally we should be punished if said mistake was...done on purpose.

I didn't want to believe that he was dead, but after receiving a picture of his decapitated head from an unknown source, I eventually had to come to terms with it. After years of my father trying to track him down, he'd finally succeeded. The Bull's entire empire had fallen, leaving me leaderless.

After the tragic death of Maggie's father, I had no other choice but to return to my beloved family. Before you start judging me on the decision of going back there, I had my reasons. Trust me, I'd rather jump in a blazing fire than go back to my father, but that's where Maggie was. With him. If I had any chance of helping her escape, then it was better to be under the same roof as her.

As a promise to her deceased father, I would get her out of that hell hole and I'd do it even if I had to risk my own life. Even if I had to kill my own brothers, I'd make sure to get her out of there, but I hope it wouldn't come to that. They probably hated me for what I did and I didn't blame them, but they were my brothers. We were of the same blood.

After mourning, I eventually bought a plane ticket from Monaco airport and traveled overnight to Hong Kong where I'm currently sitting in the lounge with my little brother. Unscathed.

Confused? Me too.

I thought when I approached the villa, I'd be shot on sight after what I'd done, but nothing happened. I didn't know what would await me when I came back, but I didn't expect this. I thought for sure that I'd be welcomed with a knife to my throat, but that wasn't the case at all. For all I knew, my brothers could be onto me, planning to kill me once I step foot inside the villa and afterward, dump my body in the sea. But it was as though I had never left. I was still being treated like royalty which fuelled my curiosity of why I was being treated as though I had done nothing wrong. I mean, I had betrayed my own family. So, why had they not confronted me or began torturing me for answers? How was I still alive?

I took a drag from my cigarette, holding the filter between my thumb and middle finger and smiled amusingly at my little brother. "*Xiǎngniàn wǒ*?" **(Miss me?)**

Kang scoffed. “Why ask a stupid fucking question, brother? I've been losing my shit being stuck here with Yuta and these sluts. You'd think they've never had any cock by how desperate they are. You better watch out they don't pounce on you, brother.”

I mean, I could understand the Yuta part.

I chuckled. “I thought you liked the company of whores?”

He gave a cynical laugh. “I do but after a while using the same ones gets boring, you know?” He leant forward in his chair and raised a row. “I bet you had some fun with the Monegasque ladies.”

I wasn't even a little surprised he knew where I was, but why hadn't they killed me in Monaco if they knew I was there. It surprises me.

I made a face. “I wouldn't know. I didn't have any free time to do what I pleased.”

I spent most of my time with Maggie's father, spending days and nights planning and deciding how to get his daughter back, but every plan always had a what if. I wasn't going to risk the lives of innocent men. I knew my father's tricks.

Kang guffaws. “*Shénme*? **(What?)** You're telling me you haven't fucked anyone in two weeks? I bet your cock has forgotten its purpose.”

I chuckled. "You have no idea. I've got the worst case of blue balls I've ever had."

He motioned to the direction of the quarters. "Then, take one of the whores to your room and give her a good fuck."

I hadn't come here to sleep with the girls. I'd come here only to rescue Maggie. That was the only reason I was here, but he didn't need to know that.

I shook my head. "*Méiyǒu.* **(No)** I'm far too tired for that."

He exhaled a plume of smoke while rolling the cigarette in his fingers. "I don't blame you. The journey must've been long for you."

I peered at him and held my breath, waiting to see if he'll elaborate, but he didn't.

Why wasn't he asking me about what I'd been doing? This was so unlike Kang. Why wasn't he grilling into me about my betrayal?

I put out my cigarette and stood up. "*Shì*, **(Yes)** it was. I'm very tired from it so I think I'm going to rest for a while."

Kang also stood. "*Děngdài.* **(Wait)** Aren't you going to say hello to Yuta? I'm sure he'll be thrilled to see you."

I wasn't a fool. I knew without a doubt Yuta would

interrogate me about my return, and I knew he'd use violence while doing it too.

I ran a hand over my slick hair and exhaled. “I'm sure he has tons of questions for me but no, not today. Knowing him, he's probably busy. I'll see him tomorrow.”

Kang eyed me. “You're not scared, are you?”

“Why would I be scared?” I asked.

He thinks for a moment then waved himself off. “*Suànle ba.*” **(Forget it)** I don't know why I said that. Have a good rest, big brother.”

I gave him a nod and a small bow, then headed to my room in the villa. I leave the lounge without a backward glance to hopefully catch sight of Maggie, but I wouldn't get my hopes up.

Armed men stood in every entrance and exit of the villa. I meet their stares with nods as I pass. Most of the rooms were empty until I came to a long hallway where to the right is an outdoor pool. There were people outside. People I recognized as my father's friends and businessmen. I take a step out and stand between the archway to peer at the girls in their company. Music played next to the bar area where two girls were dancing erotically with one another. One of the girls had a short red bob with caramel skin and the other had bright blonde hair.

My attention is drawn to the sounds of what sounded like someone diving into the pool. The pool was surrounded by people. Drunk people. The end of the pool came up to the cliff's edge where I saw two other girls kissing. I recognize them straight away. One of them was Shuang and the other girl was Ling.

Ling...

I couldn't tear my eyes away from her. Even now my heart breaks for that girl.

I remember the day I first saw her. She was drugged out of her mind, stripping her clothes off in front of middle-aged men. She didn't know where she was.

I had stumbled upon the place by chance while I was spying on one of my father's enemies. I was watching the man who was sitting a few inches from me when my attention was drawn to the girl on stage. She was pale and horribly thin. I could see the outline of her bones, and felt pitiful.

I looked at the men in the club and they had this predatory glint in their eyes. I knew at that moment that I had to save her. I couldn't watch her on that stage any longer. I decided right then and there that after her performance, I would offer her an out. I didn't think she'd accept my proposal, but she did. Without a second thought.

Back then, I thought bringing her to my father's villa

was a great idea, but now I wish that I hadn't bothered. I deeply regret my decision to bring her here, and I tell her that whenever I see her, but she never listens. All she tells me is that she's grateful that I saved her, but I can't help but think that I helped her escape one hell and brought her to another.

I take one long look at her then, continue my way in the direction of my room. It takes no little more than five minutes.

As soon as I reach my room, I close the door behind me, rest the back of my head on the door and take a deep breath.

"What the fuck are you doing, Chen?" I murmured to myself.

The same question hasn't stopped circling my mind. That's all I've been able to think about.

What if coming here was a complete and utter waste of time? For all I know she could be dead. Her colorful choice of words and her temper were probably the things that got her there.

To stop my train of thought, I go to the windows and stretch the curtains wide, revealing a set of French doors. I open the doors and step out onto the columned balcony into the salted sea breeze.

Immediately, I'm bombarded with thoughts of Maggie.

She's alive.

“She has to be.” I whispered.

Please...

“I'm a little heartbroken you didn't come and greet me, little brother.”

I jolted in surprise when I heard a voice come from behind me.

The second I heard his voice, my heart was in my throat.

Yuta.

I take another breath, exhale and slowly turn around, with a glare pointed at my big brother. “Well, the last time we saw each other, you shot me and it missed my heart within an inch. Don't be so disheartened that I'm not happy to see you, brother. You're the last person I want to see.”

He thrusts a finger at me. “And you're the last person I want to see. I haven't forgotten what you did. About your betrayal.”

I go back inside my room, closing the French doors behind me. “We all make mistakes.”

I'll never forgive him for that. Just like he won't forgive me for choosing the side of the enemy. We were both stubborn and we were both as bad as each other.

He gives me a once-over, unsmiling. “What are you doing here?”

“*Wǒ yǒu wǒ de lǐyóu.*” I nonchalantly. **(I have my reasons)**

He arched a brow. “And what would those reasons entail? It's not because of a certain girl, is it?”

Yes.

I waved him off. “No. My reason for coming back here is to apologize. I made a mistake and I'm sorry.” I lied.

Yuta's face remains immobile for a few seconds then he chuckled. “You must think I'm a fool, Chen. *Wǒ zuótiān méi chūshēng.*” **(I'm not stupid)**

“I didn't say you were.”

“You shouldn't have come back here.” He uttered.

I stared blankly at him. “You're not happy I'm back?”

His eyes narrowed on me. “What kind of question is that?”

“Kang seemed happy to see me. Seems like the only person who isn't glad to see me is you.” I said.

Yuta studied me then shook his head. “You're right, I'm not glad. In fact, I liked it better when you weren't here.

He walks towards me, his hands in his pockets. “And I

don’t accept your apology. You’re not welcome here.”

I squinted my eyes. “That's not really up to you though, is it? This is my family just as much as it is yours."

He walked forward in rage and punched me in the face, busting my lip. “Maybe you should've thought about that before choosing to side with the fucking enemy."

I fell to the ground and lied there for a moment.

“You're brave for coming back here, Chen. Very brave.”

I sighed in annoyance. “I wanted out, brother. Maybe one day, you might end up doing the exact same thing.”

“I'd never do that.” Yuta gritted out. “I'd never betray my own family.”

I stood up, wiping my lip in the process and stand toe to toe with him. Although we were about the same height, he could take me in a fight. There wasn't a time where I'd ever been able to defeat him. Even when we were kids, he always won.

“I said I was sorry. What more could you possibly want from me?” I asked.

He looked at me in distaste, then plants his fist right in my nose, breaking it. He then tackled me to the ground and started pounding his fists in my face. I taste and smell the hideous metallic taste of blood and grimace.

I gather all the strength I can muster and push him off of me. I'm surprised that for once I get the upper hand. I roll away only to go back towards Yuta and sit on his abdomen. Without any hesitation, I bring my fist back and plummet it in his face. Before I can punch him again, somebody pulls me off of him and drops on the ground.

Kang.

He stands between us, his nostrils flaring and his fists clenched. "Have you both lost your fucking minds!? Your brothers!"

"Not anymore ,we're not." I gritted out as I stood up.

Yuta also stands, his eyes swollen from my fist. "You're dead to me."

Kang swings his head in Yuta's direction. "Yuta!"

Ignoring our younger brother, he shoves him aside and marches towards me. "Tell me the real reason why you're here and I promise I won't hurt you!"

I thrust my chin out and square my shoulders. "You really think I'm going to believe that? I bet you've been wanting to kill me ever since you saw me, huh?"

Yuta growled. "*Huídá wǒ de wèntí*!" **(Answer my question)**

“No, I won't answer your question because.” I bring up my index finger and poke him in the chest. “I don't owe anything to you, much less an explanation. The only person I should explain myself to is, father. Not you.”

A pause.

Yuta looks at me in disgust. “That's one thing I'll always regret not doing.”

I frown. “What? What do you regret not doing?”

He doesn't answer me.

“Yuta?” I ask.

“I'll ask you one more time, why are you back here?”

I look him dead in the eyes. “I'm here because I wanted to apologize for taking the side of the enemy.”

Yuta's voice rises and wraps his hand tightly around my throat. “That's bullshit! You're not fucking sorry! I know exactly why you're here. It's because of her.”

“Who?” I ask while knowing exactly what the answer is going to be.

He leans into my face while squeezing my neck tighter. “Maggie. That's why you're here. You're here to take her from me.”

“You're wrong, brother.” I croaked.

“Shut the fuck up.” He takes out a knife from

somewhere and puts it against my throat. “You better watch your back because I'm on to you. You're up to something. I fucking know it.”

I shake my head. “I'm not up to anything.”

Lies.

“My gut instinct tells me that you're lying and I always trust my instincts. They're never wrong.”

“*Yěxǔ zhè cì.*” I mutter. **(Maybe this time they are)**

“They're never fucking wrong!” He looks me up and down and snarls. “I'm going to find out what you're up to, Chen because I know you're not back here to play happy families.”

“Yut...” Kang calls out his name.

But he's cut off. “Blood or not, I'll kill you. I'll slit your throat just like I did to your boss.”

My eyes widened at his declaration.

Yuta killed The Bull?

Yuta smirks. “From your reaction, I guess you didn't know.” He brings the knife up into my line of vision, “It was me, and it was this knife I used on him. I'll use it on you too when I find out exactly what you're up to, and I promise you I'll give you a proper send-off.”

He puts the knife away and releases me. I expect him to punch me or use any kind of violence on me as a warning, but he doesn't. He just leaves. As he goes, he doesn't spare me another glance as he exits my room, but his words do.

"Nice to see you too, brother." I whispered.

"He didn't tell father about you, you know." A voice says from behind me.

I turned around to see my younger brother still in my room. "*Shénme*?" **(What?)**

"Yuta. He didn't tell father about you joining the side of the enemy. He did consider telling him on multiple occasions, but he didn't." Kang said.

"*Wèishéme*?" I asked in confusion. **(Why?)**

Why hadn't Yuta told Li Wei what I had done?

It didn't make sense.

Kang shrugged. "*Wǒ bù zhīdào*. **(I don't know)** There was a time when we were having drinks on the day we came back to Hong Kong and he asked Yuta where you were. I was worried that he'd tell him the truth, and for a second, I thought he was going to tell him about you, but he didn't." Kang chuckles. "I was so shocked that he lied to our father. I could've hugged him right there. Hell, I could've kissed him."

Yuta was the type of person who didn't trust anybody or cared about anyone. He doesn't even trust his own blood, as you already know.

So, why had Yuta lied to our father about my betrayal?

"He lied to our father?" I asked.

"*Shì.*" **(Yes)** Kang nodded.

I knit my brows, unable to understand why Yuta hadn't told the truth when he obviously hated me. *"Zhēn de ma*?" **(Really?)**

Kang snorts. "I don't know whether father truly believed him, but Yuta said that you were on vacation. That you were having a break after what happened in America."

"And he believed that?"

Kang nodded.

I scoffed. "Even I wouldn't believe that. I mean, if I was father and I was told that, I'd be very suspicious."

"Yuta did what he thought was right. And he saved your ass."

I nod. "*Wǒ zhīdào*." **(I know)**

Kang approaches me. "Look, I don't know what your true intentions are for coming back here, but I hope you're not here to betray us again."

"I'm not going to betray you." I lied. "You're my brother and so is Yuta. I made a mistake, Kang and I'm sorry." I bow to show that my apology is sincere.

I hear a sigh. "Please don't betray us, brother. Not

again."

Still bowing, I close my eyes and pray that harm won't come to my brothers.

Chapter 12

Chen

The sun was beginning to set when a light knock sounded on my door. After my encounter with my brothers, I took a nap due to jet-lag and had only just now wokeup. Topless and ragged, I make my way over to my door and opened it.

I was taken aback to whom I saw.

Ling.

I greeted her with a smile. “Well, look who it is. Long time no see.”

She bowed as she greeted me. “Good evening, sir.”

I refrained myself from recoiling at what she called me. I hated it when the girls call me that. But then, I hated everything about this place.

I shake it off, place a finger gently under her chin and lift it up. “You may look at me.”

“Thank yo...” She slowly brings up her head and immediately her eyes zero in on my chest.

I chuckled nervously. “I should've put something on before opening the door. I apologize.”

“No.” She blinked repeatedly then quickly looked to the side. “I apologize, sir. I didn't mean to make you uncomfortable.”

“You didn't.” I whisper softly.

“Again, I apologize.”

I lowered my eyes and smiled amusingly. “Ling, you didn't make me uncomfortable or offend me. Just come inside and we can talk properly.”

She warily meets my eyes again and shakes her head. “Sir, I'm only here to give you a message...”

I cut her off with a frown. “Who sent you?”

She answered immediately. “Your brother.”

No doubt it was Yuta.

I opened the door and step aside. “Come inside. Whatever my brother's message is, I'm sure it can wait. Besides, I'd like to catch up with you first.”

Ling thinks for a moment, then cautiously walks into my room. I close the door behind her and grab my robe that hangs behind it.

“Have you been well?” I asked while tying the belt loosely around my waist.

I'm met with silence.

“Ling?”

I notice after a few seconds that she doesn't answer my question. I turn around to see her looking around my room.

I approach her and touch her elbow. “How many times do I need to tell you? You can relax in my room. There are no cameras here.”

She wraps her arms around herself. “How can you be so sure?”

I remove my hold on her and approach the french doors. “None of us have cameras in our rooms.”

“No?”

“No. You can talk freely.” I open the doors and step out into the evening breeze with Ling following closely behind me. “Surprisingly, father respects our privacy. You know this already.”

“I know, but I'm always afraid that I'm being watched when I'm actually not.”

I rest my back against the balcony railing. “I can assure you that you're not being watched here. It's only you and I in this room right now. Nobody else. Now, drop the pleasantries and speak to me like you would a friend.”

“It's hard.” She whispers as she closes her eyes.

“I know it's hard, but you can talk to me here. Shout at me if you want to if that'll make you feel better.”

A pause.

When she comes to stand beside me, I nudge her. “Come on, I haven't seen you in over a month. From one friend to another, do you have any gossip?”

She opens her eyes as her face saddens. “You know, I didn't have any friends before coming here. The girls here are the only friends I've ever had.”

Lies.

“Well, that's not true, is it?”

She frowned.

Does she not remember?

Well, she was on drugs at the time.

I scoff. “Well, wasn't it me who was your first friend?”

At that, she smiles. “You're not my friend, Chen. You're special. You're my saviour.” She wraps her arms around my waist and hugs me.

Was I truly her saviour?

Because I definitely didn't feel like one.

I wrapped my arms around her and held her close to my chest. “That may be so, but I still regret my decision in bringing you here.”

“Why?”

I sighed. “You know why, Ling.”

She tutted. "If it wasn't for you, I probably wouldn't be alive."

I lowered my head and shook it.

Ling cupped both of my cheeks and continued. "I know that you feel somewhat responsible for me, but you can be rest assured that I'm fine. Truly, I am."

I separated myself from her and looked at her in surprise. "Don't tell me you actually like it here?"

She couldn't be serious.

She nodded once. "Can't you see that I'm happy?"

I studied her face and as much as I hated to admit it, she did look really happy. The happiest I'd ever seen her.

She walked in the middle of the room with her arms outstretched. "I have a roof over my head, I get fed every day and I've got lovely company. What more could I want?"

It was like my mouth had a mind of its own. "Freedom?"

She turned to face me and shook her head. "I don't want it."

She didn't?

"No? Why?" I asked in curiosity.

She immediately blushed. "...Because I won't be able

to see you."

Not this again...

I lowered my head and exhale. "Ling..."

"I know!" Her voice hardened. "I don't need you to keep reminding me of why we can't be together. I've just never felt like this for somebody before, and I'm not prepared to stop feeling this way."

A pause.

"Don't you feel the same way, Chen?" She asked.

I looked over at her in dread. "I've always known about your feelings for me, but because of who I am and what my family's done to you, I couldn't do it."

"That wasn't my question." She whispered.

"What do you want me to say?"

She whimpered. "I want you to say that you like me back and that the reason why you brought me here was to actually get to know me."

She looked at me, waiting for my answer, but I couldn't bring myself to say what she wanted to hear. Of course, I liked her, but not in the way she wanted.

"You can't say it, can you?" She muttered.

I release a heavy exhale. "Ling..."

I noticed that her eyes were brimming with tears. "I

know why you don't want to be with me. You're just afraid of being with someone who's a whore."

What?

I shook my head. "That's not it..."

She cut me off. "A whore that's slept with hundreds of men. God, you must think I'm a slu..."

"Ling!" She gasped as she realised that I was standing right in front of her. "You couldn't be more wrong."

A single tear rolled down her cheek. "Then, why? Am I not good enough for you?"

"You're perfect." I gently cupped her cheek.

"If that's so, then why am I not good enough for you?"

Another pause.

She sniffled. "Chen?"

"The reason why I can't give you my heart is because it already belongs to somebody else."

Another tear rolled down her cheek.

I brushed her tears away with my thumb. "I'm sorry if my words have hurt you, and I'm sorry if I've given you false signals. It wasn't my intention to make you fall for me."

"But I have fallen for you. I've fallen for you hard." She whimpers. "I fell for you a long time ago, and ever since then I haven't looked at another man."

"Ling..."

She whimpered. "I'm in love with you, Chen. Have been for a long time. Even when I'm serving men, I can't stop thinking about you."

Is it possible she could be suffering from Stockholm Syndrome?

"What does she have that I don't?" She pleaded.

I dropped my hand. "Don't be like that."

Her face changed to guilt. "I'm sorry."

"It's fine, Ling."

"No." She leant away from my touch. "I shouldn't have asked that. I had no right."

I half shrugged. "You were curious. It's alright to be curious."

She smiled softly. "I am curious about her. Very."

My eyes widened. "You are?"

She nodded in response.

"Why?" I asked.

She rolled her eyes. "Because she's gotten your attention obviously."

"That she has."

“So, what's she like?” She asked.

A smile automatically appeared on my face while thinking about her. “She's tough. And she's crazy.”

Real fucking crazy...

Ling smiled adoringly at me. “Well, you must really like her if she makes you smile like that. I've never seen you look so happy, Chen.”

I nodded in confirmation. “I am happy but the situation is complicated.”

“I'm sure you'll figure it out. You always do.”

I gave her a wink. “We'll see. Now, what is it that my brother wanted?”

“Ah, yes. Your father has heard of your return and would like you to accompany him to dinner.”

Dinner with Li Wei.

I'd rather do anything but, a man's got to do what a man's got to do.

“I'll be there.”

She nodded and bowed, turning to leave.

Was she going? Already?

“Are you leaving?”

She turned back towards me. “Yes.”

“Must you go? We haven't had a chance to catch up.”

She smiled but it didn't reach her eyes. “I better go back. And don't worry, I'm sure there'll be another time for us to catch up.”

I wasn't so sure about that. Besides, I was only here for one thing and as soon as I had it within my grasp I was getting the two of us out of here. As soon as I was out of this place, I wasn't going to look back in dejection because I sure as hell wouldn't miss it or anyone else inside of it. Yes, even Ling.

I gave her a convincing smile. “Yeah...”

She dropped her eyes, bowed again and leaves. “Sir.”

“Ling.” I bowed my head and watched her leave silently with a blank expression.

I really hated myself sometimes.

****

The moment Ling left, I washed, dressed in a three-piece suit and made my way through the villa, feeling incredibly anxious to see my father.

He was sitting at the head of the table, with a glass of whiskey in one hand and a cigar in the other. At first, I thought he was the only person in the room, but as I get closer, I see that some of my father's close friends and business partners are also in attendance. Also in attendance was Yuta and Kang.

I had thought it was only going to be the two of us. At least, that's what I thought Ling meant. Being in the company of these people wasn't a problem for me. I'm actually pleased that I'm not alone with my father.

Really pleased.

I enter the room with a bow to my father and go to sit in my seat, next to Kang and opposite Yuta.

Dinner was mostly spent with father discussing business with his partners and talking golf with his close friends. Dinner was very pleasant because there wasn't any need for my input during the conversations. Why? The first rule while having dinner is, you do not speak until you're spoken to by, of course, Li Wei.

Every so often, the girls from the quarters would enter the room bringing in full bottles of wine and then stay for a bit to mingle with the guests before leaving again. I made sure to keep an eye out for Maggie, but there's been no sign of her bright blue hair.

Not yet, anyway.

Still, I mustn't lose hope. Perhaps she's simply resting after a night of serving customers.

I hope that isn't the case...

"My boy, Chen." My father suddenly says. "I hear that you were on vacation."

I glance in Yuta's direction to see him glaring at me over his wine glass.

I set down my fork and wipe the corners of my mouth with a napkin. "That's right, sir. I was." I confirm.

"Where did you go?" Li Wei asks.

I keep a neutral look on my face as I think of another place other than Monaco, but my mind goes completely blank. The last thing I want to do is raise suspicion by saying that I was in the same country as Maggie's father during his murder.

My father's voice changes to annoyance. "Chen? I asked you a question."

I bow my head. "*Duìbùqǐ.*" **(I'm sorry)**

I say the first thing that comes to mind.

"Where did you go?" Li Wei repeats, his tone impatient.

"*Měiguó.*" I lied. **(America)**

Li Wei frowns. "The United States?"

I nod. "*Shì.*" **(Yes)**

"You stayed there?"

"*Shì.*" **(Yes)** I answered.

"Why did you stay there after the shootout? Why didn't you come to Hong Kong with your brothers immediately?"

I bite my tongue, disappointed with myself for not being prepared for his questions.

I take a much-needed breath and exhale. "I wanted to stay a bit longer and see more of what America had to offer." I look over at Yuta to see him staring at me in hatred. "And I know I should've left with the others, and for that I'm sorry."

"What was your excuse?" Father asked.

"My excuse?" I let the question hang in the air.

Kang suddenly scoffs. "Look at him, he can't even remember. He probably spent his days drinking and spending his nights with American women."

Did Kang just...save my ass?

I swirl my head over next to me and give Kang a small bow with my head to show him my gratitude. He in return bows his head.

"Kang, I did not ask you to speak." Li Wei warns. "I asked the question to your brother. Not you. Listen."

Immediately, my younger brother bows his head. "*Duìbùqǐ.*" **(I'm sorry)**

Father sighs. "Chen, what was your excuse for not coming back with your brothers?"

What can I say other than going with what Kang said?

So, with a grin I play along. "As Kang said, I spent my days in America drinking and whoring."

My words seemed to make my father very happy. "That is all a man needs these days is a glass of whiskey to drown his sorrows in and a woman to keep his bed warm."

As my father begins to chuckle, all of his guests join in with him.

"He's definitely his father's son." Li Wei raises his glass to me to which I also do.

As the laughter simmers, one of my father's guests speaks up. "I've always wondered what the women are like in the US."

I put down my glass. "They're very beautiful, but they're nothing compared to the women here. In America, they are more ferocious and they're complete animals in the sheets. No, I prefer my women docile. That way I can do whatever I want."

Kang raises his glass. "Amen."

"Amen." I murmur.

I was relieved when the conversation turned back to business because not only did it give me the chance to breathe and think but to look out for Maggie. There was still no sign of her.

Maggie, where are you?

****

An hour later and our dishes were cleared away from the table.

On one end of the table, Li Wei was gathered around his friends and business partners, while on the other end sat my brothers.

Yuta had yet to say anything. He'd remained silent throughout the whole evening.

"Are you two just going to sit there and not say anything to each other?"

Neither Yuta nor I answered him.

"*Wǒ wú huà kě shuōle.* **(I have nothing to say)** Both of you know this."

Again, we remain silent.

"Chen?" Kang asks.

My mouth remains shut.

Kang waits for a few seconds but then turns his attention to our older brother. "Yuta?"

"I've got nothing to say to him." Yuta says with a deadpan expression.

He had nothing to say?

I shrugged. “Neither have I.”

Yuta points his finger at me. “You've got a lot of explaining to do, mainly the fact of why you're back here, but you're choosing not to answer truthfully.”

“I have said all the things I needed to say.” I grit out.

He makes a noise at the back of his throat. “Stop lying. Just tell me what the fuck you're up to.”

I sighed in frustration. “I've told you...”

Yuta slams the table with his fist. “And I'm choosing not to believe that. Tell me the truth! What are you hiding?”

“Nothing, brother.” I murmured. “I've told you everything you wanted to know.”

He looks at me in disgust, then shoves himself away from the table, storming out of the room, leaving me and Kang completely stunned.

“Why can't you just say what he wants to hear?” Kang says.

I raise my glass and drain the contents inside. “And what would that be?”

He looked solemnly into my eyes. “You're here for the girl, aren't you? Otherwise, you wouldn't be here.”

At that moment, a girl with a red bob sits on Kang's

lap. She leans into Kang's ear and they both chuckle. He rubs his palm along the whore's thigh and points his blue eyes at me. “I'm up for it if Chen is.”

“Up for what?” I asked.

Kang holds up a clear plastic baggie with white contents inside. “What do you say?”

“Kang.” I warned.

He rolled his eyes. “*Shénme*?” **(What?)**

“What's that?” I ask although I already know what it is.

He tutted. “You know exactly what this is, brother.”

Enraged, I snatched the bag of coke from him. “You're still doing this shit?”

He snatched it back from me. “It's good shit. Plus, I feel like we're going to be here for a while. So, why not do a couple of lines with me?”

“I'm not doing it and I'd rather you didn't do it either.” I demand. “I don't want you to overdose.”

But he ignored me.

I watch as he takes a line of cocaine for himself, then uses his finger to run along across the powder and bring it up for the girl on his lap to inhale. She breathes it in and moans in delight.

“You still haven't answered me, brother.”

I cast him a glance. “I'm not here for the girl.”

He shakes his head. “*Shuōhuǎng zhě*.” **(Liar)**

“*Hēi*!” **(Hey!)** I say defensively. “Don't call me a liar when I'm telling you the truth.”

He shrugged. “It's just my opinion.”

I clicked my tongue. “You sound just like Yuta.”

He shoves the whore away with a slap to the ass then brings his chair closer to mine. “Just tell me, brother, what are your intentions for coming here?”

“I've told you my intentions, Kang. I'm here because I made a mistake.”

“You still fucked up. You fucked up bad. And I agree with Yuta. You're brave for coming back here and a little bit stupid. I'll admit that it's nice to have you back here, but I can't help but think that you're up to something.”

I scoffed. “Not you too, Kang.”

“All I'm saying is that we wouldn't be in this situation right now if it wasn't for that blue haired bitch.”

I close my eyes. “Watch your mouth.”

“But it's true, otherwise, none of this would've happened.”

“Oh well, they say everything happens for a reason.”

“That they do.” Kang lowers his voice. “But just tell me, brother. She's the reason you're here, isn't it?”

“No, it's...”

He cut me off. “Don't give me that crap. You might as well tell me what the fuck you're up to because I'm high as a fucking kite right now. I probably won't remember this conversation. Get whatever's off your chest.”

Pause.

“Chen?”

All that kept going through my mind was if I should tell him the truth or not.

“You're not here to see me or Yuta. Not really. And you're definitely not here for father. You're here for Maggie.”

I shrugged. “So what if I am? How is it any different to what you're doing?”

Kang frowned.

“I know all about your history with Shuang.”

“Who doesn't?” He said nonchalantly.

“As far as I've heard, you've not laid with anyone since coming back from America. You fuck everything with a pulse, but yet when Shuang is near, you don't touch another woman.”

He peered at me. “Your point?”

My eyes widened. “Could this be love, brother?”

“Love?” He scoffed. “I don't know the meaning of the word.”

I shook my head. “Wrong. I see the way you look at her and watch her when she walks away. That's love, brother.”

“Stop saying that word.” He demanded.

“If you want me to stop, just admit it.” I smiled amusingly.

“No.”

With a huge grin on my face, I put up my hands in surrender. “Fine. Deny it all you want, but deep down you know I'm right.”

He bends down his head, snorts another line and growls as he sits up again. “ And what's the big deal, anyway? Who cares if I like her?”

“If you love her, why are you letting other guys fuck her?”

I watched him as he thinks over my words.

“Kang?”

He snapped. “What?”

I lowered my voice. “Wouldn't you rather have her all

to yourself?"

He remains silent.

"Imagine having her all to yourself, every night of every day. Just you and her fucking like there's no tomorrow. Tell me you haven't thought about that?"

Because I had. More than once.

With Maggie.

"Kang?"

Pause.

He nods slowly. "I thought about it a long time ago, but this family means more to me than just some whore. Whores are replaceable. Families aren't."

I repeat his words inside my head and all of a sudden I'm overcome with guilt.

"Ah, look who it is, brother." Kang points towards the archway. "I was wondering when she'd make an entrance."

I follow Kang's finger that's pointed towards the doorway where a head of bright blue hair entered the room, holding a bottle of rare whiskey.

Shit.

She was here.

"She's alive." I mutter under my breath.

I held my breath as my heart accelerated inside my chest. I couldn't look away from her as she made her way over to Li Wei. She was wearing a black bodysuit corset with black stilettos.

Just the pure sight of her made me excited, but I kept a straight face. Her head remained lowered to the ground, making it impossible for her to see me.

“She's really here.” I mutter under my breath.

Next thing I hear is Kang chuckling. “You're such a liar. You are here for her.”

I tear my eyes away and land them on Kang. I couldn't make out his expression. Nor could I bring myself to say anything.

“What?” I ask.

He motions to my face. “Your face says it all, brother. I watched you when she came in here, and your face lit up. Maybe I'm wrong. Maybe it's the cocaine making me see shit.”

“It's the cocaine, brother.” I muttered.

When my gaze finds Maggie again, I'm unable to look away from her. She was no longer the feisty, strong girl I remembered her to be. No, she was the complete opposite of that now. Maybe it was all just an act, but I didn't like this look on her. Not one bit. It didn't suit her.

I wanted to see the fire in her eye and the fight in her body, but it was as though all the strength inside of her had gone.

This place had done that to her.

“Whore with the blue hair!” Kang shouts. “Come over here.”

With her head still lowered, she advances towards us, and as she does, it makes me get a better look at her.

I hate what they've done to her. She'd lost weight. Thanks to this place, she looked fragile and delicate. A look I most definitely did not like on her.

But even now, looking the way she is, she still manages to arouse me. It sickens me. Her father would be far from happy if he knew the thoughts of what I wanted to do to his daughter.

I'm sorry.

Shame flooded inside my chest, but my eyes refused to look at anything else other than her. I wanted to reach out and run my hands through her hair.

Come closer...

Before I could even lay a finger on her, Kang beat me to it. My jaw tensed when I see him dragged Maggie by the arm and placed her on his lap.

“You may raise your head.” Kang commanded.

I held my breath as the words left Kang's mouth. I wondered what her reaction would be when she saw me. As she slowly brought up her head, our eyes collided with one another and everything froze. Her eyes widened in recognition as the shock registered on her face.

Why was she so surprised to see me? Did she perhaps think I was dead after what happened the last time she saw me?

Her emerald, green eyes bore into mine, completely taking my breath away.

“Aren't you going to say hello to her, brother?” Kang asks as cups her cheek.

Pause.

“Chen?”

I look at the hand that's currently touching her in distaste. “I will after you remove your hand.”

At that, Maggie gives me a death glare.

“*Wèishéme*? **(Why?)** Does it make you jealous?” Kang provokes.

And that’s when reality sank in.

I was here for one thing and one thing only. The last thing I want to do is let my jealousy get the better of me and jeopardize this mission.

With one final glance at Maggie, I clear my throat and stand up. "*Láojià.*" **(Excuse me)**

I don't wait to see what my brother says and head for the exit when a voice stops me.

"You're retiring for the evening already?" My father asks from the other side of the room.

I'm left feeling a little unsettled at the way he looks at me.

Shit!

Did Yuta tell him?

I turn to face him and bow. "Yes, father."

He frowns. "But it's still early."

"Indeed, but I'm still a little tired after the flight."

"Ah, yes." Li Wei nods. "Very well. I shall see you in the morning."

Dismissed, I bow again and head to my room.

By the time I reached my room, I was tired and anxious to see what tomorrow would bring. After recent events, I was beginning to feel whether coming back here was a good idea.

I hoped that I'd chosen wisely.

I go to sleep that night with one thing on my mind.

Maggie.

I need to get her out of here and return her to her grieving mother who is no doubt worried sick. Getting her out of this hell was the only thing keeping me going. Besides, I was only a few steps closer to bringing her home.

Chapter 13

Chen

I woke up the next morning with a goal in mind; to get Maggie the fuck out of here. To do that, I must first approach Maggie and fill her in on everything, but how was I going to get her alone with watchful eyes watching my every move.

I didn't want to stay here longer than I needed to, but before I could even think of doing anything related to this mission, I needed food. I had to keep my energy up, especially for this kind of mission. I took a shower, dressed in a black suit, and shaved. I had to look sharp, especially in front of my father.

I shortly left my room and followed the scent of cigar smoke and the sound of people talking. It led me outside to the poolside veranda where I immediately spot my father talking to a sharply dressed man. No doubt they were talking business.

Just as I edged nearer to them, father's business partner suddenly comes to a stand, bowed, and excused himself, giving me a small nod as he passed.

I stood by the edge of father's table and bowed. "*Zǎoshang hǎo.*" **(Good morning)**

Li Wei looked out of the tall glass windows and slowly nodded. "A good morning it is." He motioned to the chair opposite him. "*Zuò xià.*" **(Sit down)**

I took a seat just as the kitchen staff brought out different bowls of fruits and juices to the table.

"Did you sleep well?" Father asked.

I nodded. "Yes, thank you. Although I had a great time in America, nothing beats coming home. What's that saying? There's no place like home?"

"That there isn't, but I wish to go back there someday. America."

"For what reason?" I asked.

Li Wei grinned. "The pussy obviously."

The two of us shared a chuckle, but mine was more forced.

"Here, son." My father hands me a cigar to which I gladly accept with a polite thank you.

"Is everything alright? Business going well?" I asked as I poured myself a glass of orange juice.

"*Cónglái méiyǒu gèng hǎo de.*" **(Never better)** He answered with a smirk.

I hated the fact that things were going so well for him. More than anybody, I wanted to see his empire crumble to the ground once and for all.

"That's good to hear, father." I put on a false smile.

"In the end, I always win." He uttered confidently.

I noticed the faraway look in his eyes. "Was business not going well?"

He took a drag from his cigar and sneered. "Not too long ago, my cargo kept getting stolen from me. I didn't know who was taking it. Hadn't a fucking clue."

I knew. It was me.

I was the one that was secretly giving intel to Maggie's father on what my father was doing regarding shipments and such. We only did it to provoke him, and it worked, but in the end, one of us had to suffer the consequences.

"Do you know who was responsible?"

His look darkened. "Now I do."

Had he found out that I betrayed him and was involved in his cargo getting stolen? A shiver ran down my spine just at the thought of it.

"Who was it?"I casted a nervous glance at him only to see him looking at me curiously. "*Cāicè*." **(Guess)**

"Guess?" I asked.

Li Wei merely stared expectantly at me.

I answered although I knew the answer already.

I pretend to think for a moment then answered. “Well, considering he’s your biggest enemy, my guess would have to be The Bull.”

He begins to chuckle. “He thought he’d gotten away with it. Karma is indeed a bitch.”

I bit my tongue and smiled.

He tapped his cigar on the glass tray and took another inhale. “I have yet to ask Yuta how it felt to kill him.”

I clenched my fist under the table at the mention of his name.

“Happy, I bet.”

He chuckled. "I would be as well. A part of me was jealous that Yuta got the opportunity to kill ‘The Bull’. You have no idea how many men wanted him dead.”

I already knew this, but hearing it coming from my father made me feel physically sick. That man was like a father to me.

“Must be a great achievement for you. To have one of your sons killing one of the most wanted men in the world.” I muttered.

“Not only that, but we have something of his." Li Wei smirked. "Something very precious to him.”

Maggie.

I arched a brow. “You do?”

"Did you know that we have his daughter?"

Yes.

My eyes widened. "You have her here?"

"*Shì.*" **(Yes)** Li Wei grinned widely. "She was the girl that you and your brothers held hostage in America. She's here now and appeared last night at dinner. I'm surprised you didn't ask her to serve you."

"Ah, yes. Kang called her over but I retired for the evening just shortly after she came to sit with us." I said.

He nodded, unsmiling. "Quite a beautiful looking thing. She's indeed her mother's daughter."

"The Korean model?"

"Yes, but her age is starting to show."

A thought occurred to me. "Father, if I may ask, why are you still keeping her when her father has been dealt with?"

Li Wei chuckled at my question. "I was thinking that her daughter would make a very good mistress, don't you agree?"

Absolutely fucking not.

I frowned. "*Dărăo yīxià*?" **(Excuse me?)**

Li Wei grinned maliciously. "Unless you want her for yourself?"

That was the plan.

"I would like her to service me some time, but nothing more than that. Who would want to settle with a dirty rotten whore?"

As soon as the words left my mouth, I felt sick to my stomach. Obviously, the words were a lie but my father had to believe that nothing was going on between Maggie and I. If only I could meet with her privately without raising suspicion?

"Why not have her service you today?"

Oh?

I scoffed as I rolled the cigar between my fingers. "There's probably a long line of men waiting to sink in between her thighs. I will just have to wait my turn."

He sipped his drink and shook his head. "No son of mine waits, but lucky enough for you, there isn't a line of men waiting. After they heard of what she did to Sal, nobody wanted her. At least not until she's obedient."

What had she done to Sal?

"Sal?"

"She's only serviced one person and that was Sal."

I hid my grimace.

"But before he could stick his cock in her, she

knocked him out and ran away."

That's my girl.

I stifled my smile and frowned. "She's a wild one."

"That she is, but she will be tamed." He grit out.

Inside, I was laughing with glee. Nothing amused me more than seeing my father agitated.

I cleared my throat. "Was she punished for her reckless behaviour?"

He scoffed. "Of course she was punished. And her father paid the price for that. She won't do it again, otherwise, it will be her mother next."

It won't be because he'll be dead by then. Hopefully.

I grinned evilly. "Father, if she misbehaves again, let me be the one to punish her."

His eyes widened with interest. "You wish to punish her yourself?"

I nodded. "*Shì.* **(Yes)** I have not done it before and would like to try it if, of course, you would allow it."

"I have no objection to you doing it, but you'll have to beat your brother to it first."

Before I have a chance to ask him what he means by his words, he snapped his fingers and immediately a server appeared at his side.

"Take the new whore to my son's room. She is to service Chen today." He demanded.

The server bowed. "Yes, sir."

He dismissed her and turned to me. I looked at him in confusion. "She is to serve me now? Today?"

Li Wei shrugged. "Why wait? She's here to be used. She's a whore."

I remained silent because I was afraid of what I would say once I opened my mouth.

My father smirked. "I suggest you get your fill before I keep her all to myself."

In your fucking dreams.

"I'd fucking ruin that whore." Li Wei groaned.

Sickened, I clear my throat and pushed away from the table. "Therefore, I'll get right to it and use her before passing her over to you."

Hopefully, we'll be gone before that happens.

Father chuckled. "Don't tire her out too much, son."

"Yes, father." I bowed and left the table, heading directly to my room.

While walking down the corridors, all I could think about was my mission of getting Maggie out of here. I didn't want to stay here any longer. Every second I spent inside this villa was uncomfortable. I was afraid that at any moment, I would be butchered for my betrayal. The sooner I got out of here, the better. I just had to speak to Maggie and figure out a plan with her.

I knew the place inside and out, but what I didn't know was finding the right escape route that'll suit me when the time comes. I wanted to choose the safest route because I wanted both of us to make it out alive. The obvious choice of escape would be jumping off the cliff. The villa was placed on the edge of the cliff, and most of the time, it was left unguarded. All Maggie and I would have to do is jump into the ocean, but the jump itself was somewhat high.

Could Maggie make the jump knowing it might lead to her death? I won't risk her life. I just couldn't. The two of us had to make it out alive.

As I walked through the empty hallways, I couldn't help but feel like I was being watched. Maybe I was overreacting, but I always had a keen intuition for danger. I stop my movements and look behind me. Nothing.

I shook my head and continued forward until I was standing in front of my door. I took a deep breath and exhale. Knowing that Maggie was just inside this room made my heartbeat increase. Blood pumped hard throughout my body, especially in one particular area.

God, I wanted to see her. Never in my life had I wanted to see someone so badly before.

I reach for the doorknob and enter my room to see her tied up to my four-poster bed. She had been laid out for me like a gift, waiting to be unwrapped.

Her arms were stretched over her head, her wrists tied to the post. She wore nothing other than white lace underwear, and a blindfold. I closed the door behind me and advanced towards her.

"Yuta?" She asked, her chest moving rapidly in between breaths.

Was she scared? Had Yuta hurt her?

The thought of him laying a finger on her made me want to punch something.

With my eyes glued to her frame, I prowl towards her and sit by her side, quietly watching her breasts rise and fall. I could see her pink nipples through her bra, they were calling for my touch.

I had to touch her because if I didn't, I'd lose control, but I couldn't bring myself to do it. I wasn't here to make a move on her. I was here to save her from this god awful place.

And god help me I was going to do it.

"Yuta?" She asked breathlessly.

I frowned. "Why do you call for my brother?"

There's a pause and then a gasp. "Chen? Is that you?"

I smiled even though she couldn't see it. "That's right, it's me."

There's another long pause.

"I thought you were dead." She muttered.

I reached up and removed the blindfold. "Do I look dead to you?"

Her eyes were red-rimmed, and brimming with tears as she took me in. "Oh my god. I thought I was seeing things. Last night, when I saw you, I thought my mind was playing tricks on me, but it's really you."

I can't bear the sight of seeing her cry. Seeing her like this felt like someone was stabbing me in the heart.

Repeatedly.

I cup her chin with my hand, tilting her face so she had no choice but to look at me. "Did you really think a bullet was going to fucking stop me from seeing you?"

She frowned. "But I don't understand. How are you here? Alive? Unharmed...?"

I cut her off. "I'm fine. At least for now. And I arrived just a few days ago, after..."

What happened to your father...

I stopped talking when I see a tear drop from her eye, "Don't say it. Just don't. Please, I don't want to hear anyone mentioning it."

I swept along her bottom lip with my thumb. "I know you don't, but please let me say this."

She clenched her eyes shut. "Chen..."

I sighed. "I'm sorry I couldn't do anything for him. I really am sorry, Maggie. I turned my back for a second, and by the time I realised what was actually going on, he'd already been caught by my father's men." I lower my eyes. "I blame myself for what happened to him."

Maggie slowly opens her eyes. "It's not your fault. It's my fault for getting in this fucking mess in the first place."

I remove my hold. "That's why I'm here. I'm here to get you out, and take you back home where you belong."

Her face saddens. "I did manage to escape once, but because of that my father got murdered. I'm not prepared to go through that again, Chen. I can't lose my mother too."

"You won't. I promise you won't lose her because this time, you'll succeed in getting out of this place. I'm going to help you, and I'll risk my life making sure you leave this place alive."

She shakes her hand. "You won't succeed. Your family's too powerful."

"That's where I come in. I'll gain my brother's trust again and that's when we'll make our move."

She clicks her tongue. "It won't work."

"Yes, it will. I'll make sure of it."

Pause.

"How could you come back here knowing what you've done to your family? Have you lost your mind?"

"I know what I'm doing."

Her voice hardened. "It's too dangerous for you to be here. And to be seen with me. You betrayed your father and your brothers for god sakes!"

"I know what I did."

"Then, how are you still fucking standing!? How are your limbs still attached?"

I looked at her reassuringly. "Nobody knows anything except for my brothers. They think I'm back here to reconcile with them."

"And you're not here to do that?"

As if.

"Fuck no! I'm here for you. Only you."

She bit her lip, looking unsure at me.

"I'm not here to make up with my brothers. I'm here

for you."

She looked up and studied me carefully. "What about your father?"

"As far as I know, he doesn't know anything." I answered truthfully.

There's a long pause before she spoke again. "I don't trust your brothers. I don't trust them at all."

I scoffed. "You don't even know them."

Her eyes widened at that. "What did you just fucking say!? I know them enough to know that they're cruel fucking monsters!"

"Maggie..."

"Do you have any idea what I've been through!?" She shrieks.

I look at her face, see the hurt in her eyes and immediately regret my choice of words.

"I'm sorry." I say, my voice laced with shame.

"You've got no idea!"

I sigh. "I know, I'm sorry. I never should've said that. Forgive me."

She looks at me with an expressionless look then clicks her tongue. "So, are we done here?"

"I'm done talking, yes."

"Then, if we're done, are you going to let me go?" She looks up at her bound hands, then looks back at me expectantly. "Well?"

I release a shuddering breath and lean closer to her. "I don't really want to."

It was true, I didn't want to end things here. I wanted to keep her here as long as possible. Yes, even if that meant sleeping with her. Call me a selfish bastard, but I never said I was the good guy.

Did I?

"What?"

I tilt her head and gaze into her eyes. "I'm not done with you, yet."

She looks at me with a puzzled look on her face. "You're not actually going to make me service you, are you?"

I remained silent.

She gasped. "Chen..."

"I'm not going to hurt you." I said. "You don't need to be afraid of me. I just want a taste before I let you go."

Before I give her a chance to stop me, I kiss her. Her lips were soft, like velvet. I kissed her gently, they were no little more than breaths against her lips. She lets out a small moan, I catch it with my lips and whisper, "Unless you want to stay the night."

"Not a chance." Maggie whispered.

I smiled against her lips. "You disappoint me. Didn't you miss me at all?"

She scoffed. "I missed your wit, not your cock."

I regard her for a moment then sweep my eyes up and down her body. I gave her a peck. "That's too bad because my cock missed you."

At that she rolled her eyes. "Why are you doing this, Chen?"

"Because I'm selfish." I said bluntly.

A hint of a smile takes over her face as she pulls away. "No shit. You're not the only Jinyoung brother I've met, that's selfish."

The mention of my brothers stirred something inside of me. I knew one thing for certain was that I didn't like her mentioning my brothers. God knows what they've done to her.

I cleared my throat. "While you've been here, have they...?"

I let the question hang in the air.

"What? Fucked me? Abused me?" Maggie finished the question.

I made a noise at the back of my throat to confirm.

She sighed. "They brought me here as a whore. So, of

course, they're going to use me."

"Yeah, and I bet you enjoyed it as well." I grunt as I reach up and undo the ropes around her wrists.

I bet she loved all the fucking attention.

When she lowers her arms, I climb from the bed and stand facing the french doors, looking out into the ocean.

I feel her eyes on my back as I place my hands on my hips. I can do nothing other than picture her with my brothers.

"Chen?"

I tensed my jaw. "Did you come?"

There's a pause.

When I turn around, I instantly know the answer just by looking at her face. "Did. You. Come?"

She glared at me. "Yeah."

I looked at her and shook my head, causing her to peer over at me. "Why does that bother you?"

I snapped. "How could it not!?"

Another pause.

"Wait, are you jealous?" She asked.

I remained silent.

She clambers off the bed and comes towards me, with a seductive glint in her eyes. “Huh? Are you jealous that your brothers got to fuck me first?”

I glared into her green eyes. “Stop it.”

She grinned. “Are you jealous that they got to touch every inch of this body?”

“I said stop it.” I gritted out.

But she ignored me.

“Are you jealous of the fact that while they were fucking me, I enjoyed every second of it?”

Lies.

My nostrils flared. “Are you done?”

She looked up at me expectantly, then rolled her eyes. “God, you’re so pathetic.”

My eyes widened at that. “I’m what?”

Maggie sighed. “You’re getting jealous over nothing. Am I yours? No. Are we in love? Fuck no.” She thrusts her finger at my chest. “In fact, I should fucking hate you, but I don’t because you’re here to help me, unlike your fucking brothers.”

They’d never help her escape. They were too far up my father’s ass.

She grabs the collar of my shirt with both of her hands and pulls my face closer to hers. “Grow the fuck up and remember what you're here to do."

I stare down at her lips. "I will after I'm done with you."

She gasps, and suddenly I'm on her, seeking out her lips with my own. Gone was the gentleness I had pointed at her earlier because it was now replaced with need. I grab her, pull her into my arms and plant hard kisses all over her. She gasps as I lift her up, my hands gripping her hips. Maggie holds on to me, wraps her legs around my waist while her arm encircles my neck, holding on to me while I move us over to the bed.

I lay her down on the white sheets and lie down on top of her, pressing my weight down on her. Excitement soars through my body as I trail my lips from hers, down her jaw line and to her neck. I kiss, lick and graze my teeth lightly across her skin as my hand trails up her thigh and into her lacy underwear. When my fingertips graze her clit, her back arches as a gasp escapes from her throat. Without a second thought, I tear off her undergarments, and shower kisses all over her exposed skin. I circle my tongue around her nipple, feeling it tighten and perk underneath my touch. I move slowly to my knees, trailing my hands over her ass and the back of her thighs. I hated the fact that they were thin, but she was still beautiful.

Clutching her hips, I cover my mouth over her mound, causing her to cry out. I lift one of her legs and drape it over my shoulder for better access. I then use my thumbs to open her and dive in. I smile to myself when her hips buck underneath my mouth. Maggie gasps when my tongue flicks over the most sensitive spot on her body. My lips seal over the small bundle of nerves and apply pressure there with my tongue. She freezes and tenses, causing me to continue with the pressure on her clit without pause. She throws her head back as her fingers grip the sheets, while all the while filling the room with her loud moans. Her climax soon follows, making her cry out loudly. Her muscles tremble, as ripples pulsate through her shaking body.

My hands make quick work of my pants, unbuckling the belt and unzipping them, while also removing my boxers in the process. I pry open her legs and move into the space between them. Her eyes immediately zero in on my cock and widen at its length. I grasp a hold of my length and gently push inside of her, covering her entire body with mine. The second I slide myself inside her, she cries out in pleasure. I find my rhythm, and hike up Maggie's leg to fill her deeper. She gasps, running her fingers through my hair and pulls me down to kiss her. I thrust harder as our lips meet, and hear abnormal noises coming from her throat. I swallow them with my kisses and increase my pace. She cries out and arches her back again, her breasts flush against my chest as she convulses around my cock. My breath comes out in my pants as I continue thrusting until I feel my own release approaching.

As Maggie comes from her high, I pull out, sit back on my knees, throw back my head and begin stroking myself. Seconds later my release follows. I slow down my strokes and sit gazing at Maggie, my chest falling and rising as I breathe deeply.

Maggie holds my stare and scoffed. “That... can never happen again.”

Chapter 14

Maggie

When was the last time I'd been kissed like that? Kissed as though it meant something other than ownership? Never. It was...nice. But it still felt strange.

The two of us were silent as we lay next to each other, our breaths the only thing filling the silence of the room. I hated it. Hated the awkwardness of it. Didn't like it one bit.

Sitting up from the bed, I cover myself with the sheet and faced Chen. "This was a mistake. Do you understand me?"

His eyes narrowed. "Wait, what?"

I get up from the bed and start getting dressed. "You heard me. This never happened."

With a frown, he looked down at my naked body, looked at his own, then motions between the two of us. "So, this meant nothing to you? What we just did."

I still couldn't shake off this weird feeling. A feeling I couldn't quite place. Was it confusion? Love? No way...What did love feel like?

I released a heavy exhale. “It was just sex. And besides, we’re not here to mess around, Chen.” I took a look at his hurt face and frowned. “Why? Did it mean something to you?”

He looked at me as though I’d grown a second head. “Of course, it did! I don’t fuck just anybody, Maggie. I’m not like Kang or Yuta.” I watched him as he climbed off the bed and put on his boxers. “I actually give a shit about the person I sleep with.”

Was that supposed to make me feel better?

“And what? You want me to be happy about that? You want me to shout hallelujah to the sky that I allowed you to stick your cock inside of me?” I clapped mockingly. “Halle-fucking-lujah. Good for you, Chen.”

He tensed his jaw and glared at me. “You’re such a cold woman, you know that?”

“Yeah, tell me something I don’t already know.” I spat.

He studied me for a few seconds then shook his head. “You know, I thought after what we just did that it might’ve softened that ice cold heart of yours, but guess I was wrong.”

“What do you want from me!?” I shrieked.

Chen’s voice hardened as he stopped in front of me. “I

want you to stop treating me like shit and start treating me like an equal. Unless you start respecting me, I'm not going to get you out of here."

My eyes widened at the audacity. "Are you threatening me Chen? Seriously?"

He stared at me with a blank expression on his face which causes me to shove at his chest in frustration. "Answer me!"

He runs his hand through his hair as he thinks for a moment. "When your father died, I promised to myself that I was going to do anything to get you out of here, but if you keep treating me like your bitch to screw around and command, I might have to change my perspective of things."

I clicked my tongue in distaste. "You're such a turncoat. But I can't say I'm surprised. I knew the moment things got complicated that you'd change your mind about everything. You're a coward."

"I'm not a coward." Chen gritted out.

I release a whimper as I shove at his chest again. "Your only job is to get me out of here. You've been here almost a week and I'm still fucking here. I'm starting to think you've forgotten your reason for coming back here."

"I haven't forgotten anything." He said bluntly.

"Then, why haven't you done anything yet?"

He sighed. "I'm picking the right moment."

I'll be waiting forever if I don't take matters into my own hands.

"Why the fuck do I need to do everything around here?" I muttered under my breath as I reach out my hand to him. "Give me your gun and I'll get us both out of here right now."

As I say the words, the last thing I expected for him to do was to break into a smile. "What?"

"Give me your gun." I repeated.

I'll most likely but at least I died trying to get out of here.

Chen grinned. "I'm not giving you my gun."

"Give it to me." I demanded.

He stands toe to toe with me and looked down at me with amusement. "No. We're doing this my way."

Yeah, and his way sucked.

"I'll be waiting forever." I whispered.

Chen grabbed my chin and gave me a quick peck. "You won't be waiting forever. I made a vow to your father that I was going to get you out of here. And I'm sure as hell going to do it."

And just like that, I believed his words.

I shook my head and groaned. “I can’t stand it here anymore. It’s tearing me apart.”

He rest his hands on my arms and leant down. “Soon, you’ll be out of here and back with your mother and you’ll never have to walk down these halls again. But until then, endure it.”

Endure it? Until when?

There was only so much a person could take until they exploded, and I was close to breaking point. I was tired of walking on eggshells around these people while pretending to be somebody that I wasn’t. This god awful place had turned me into something I had feared of becoming -- Weak and powerless.

But this wasn’t who I was born to be. I was born a fight.

I nodded slowly to Chen and exhaled. “Fine, I’ll endure it.”

"Good girl." Chen smiled softly and winked. “You can do it.”

I nodded.

Chen nodded to the door. “Go.”

Shouldering past him, I reach for the doorknob only to jump when I see a familiar figure lingering outside. Ling.

With a curios stare, I closed the door behind me and smiled softly at her. “Hi.”

But when her eyes lock with mine, I’m taken aback to see how empty and cold they looked. A look I had never seen on Ling before. And it leaves me unsettled. Why was she looking at me like this? As though I’d hurt her.

I call her name. “Ling?”

She only stared at me without a word.

What the hell had I done to deserve this kind of attitude? I’ve done nothing wrong.

“*Gwaenchanh-a*?” I asked. **(Are you okay?)**

“Are you leaving?” Her voice was so quiet that I could only just manage to make out the words.

I blinked repeatedly. “What?”

“Leaving? Are you leaving?” Ling repeats, her words sounding harsh.

Leaving?

And then my eyes widened.

Shit!

Had she heard my entire conversation with Chen? About him helping me get out of here? God, I fucking hope not.

No, I was overreacting. She wouldn't eavesdrop, and besides Ling wouldn't snitch. She wasn't like that...Was she?

"I'm leaving the room now, yes." I utter. "I was brought here to service a customer."

Her response was instant. "How long have you been in there with the customer?"

"About half an hour." Give or take.

She doesn't bat an eyelash as she asked the next question. "What kind of service did the customer want?"

Was this an interrogation or something?

I scoffed. "What?"

She tensed her jaw and clenched her fists beside her. "Was Che...I mean, was the customer satisfied?"

What was with all the twenty questions? Why was she so interested in what I was doing with this particular customer? It shouldn't be any of her business, right?

I frowned. "Why would you ask that? What? Do you think I'm unable to satisfy a man?"

"That's not what I asked." Ling said bluntly.

My eyes widened. "You think I'm incompetent?"

I knew the girls were curious about who was serving whom, but Ling's reaction to this was a little mysterious.

She avoided my eyes as she answered. "Of course not."

"Then why....?" I let the question hang in the air.

She peered up at me with furrowed brows. "It's important that the customers here are left satisfied. And considering what you did to the last customer, I didn't want us girls to be punished again by your actions."

My stomach dropped at the bitterness of her words. I thought she was my friend, but guess I was wrong.

I plastered a fake grin on my face. "Well, maybe this time I wanted to satisfy the customer considering how attractive he was. And don't worry, he was left very satisfied. After I finished, he couldn't remember his own name." I lied.

Like a switch, her face changed to anger.

"Good, We wouldn't want to disappoint anyone, would we?" She muttered through gritted teeth.

"Well, that's for me to worry about, isn't it? It's not your problem or your business with what I do with the customers."

Shouldering past her, I leave her standing there as I walked back to the quarters with more unanswered questions swirling around my head.

****

The last time I'd been outdoors was the day of my escape. When I was captured and returned back to the villa, all I've been craving is to be outside and inhale the fresh air and feel the breeze through my hair. Sure, I would only need to take a step to feel the sun on my skin, but it wouldn't be the same as before because I was still imprisoned.

But I won't be for long.

After leaving Ling behind, I rushed back to the quarters to find Shuang waiting for me. She told me that myself, her and Shuang were needed to keep the customers entertained at the outside pool. I dressed in a white bikini and reapplied my makeup. A routine I despised doing because I always feel like a clown after putting it on my face.

As soon as I finished applying the makeup, Shuang had given me a once over and a nod of approval then accompanied me down the villa halls.

"Is Ling okay?" I asked Shuang in a low tone.

I turned my head slightly to see her frowning. "She was fine this morning. Why do you ask?"

I waved it off. "It's probably nothing, but after talking

to her, I was left feeling a little concerned."

"When was this?"

"Earlier. I was called to Chen's room this morning and when I left, Ling was standing outside of it, looking rather upset."

Shuang suddenly stops in her tracks and faces me. "Wait, you were called to Chen's room? That's where you were?"

I stopped to face her and nodded. "Yes."

She scoffed. "Can you blame her for being upset?"

I frowned. "What?"

Shuang breaks into a smile. "Please don't tell me you're that blind, Maggie?"

"What do you mean?" I asked.

With a mischievous grin, she walks away leaving me completely baffled.

With a shake of my head, I take a step forward and immediately feel the warm sun embrace my skin. I catch the scent of chlorine and body oils as I near the pool and already see Shuang kissing one of the customers.

She sure as hell doesn't waste any time.

Without batting an eye in her direction, I continue forward and sit on one of the lounge chairs, but jerk in surprise when I hear voices coming from behind me inside the veranda. I lower myself in the chair and tilt my head upwards to catch their conversation.

While one of the voices made my heart leap, the other voice made me want to squeeze the life out of something.

Li Wei.

From where I was standing, I could see the figures clearly. Li Wei was wearing a white suit, while Chen was wearing a white shirt and black shorts. Seeing him dressed so casually almost made me want to smile. Not to forget he's wearing the same white shirt he'd worn to fuck me this morning. The memory of him devouring me causes my cheeks to burn. Once again, another surge of emotion stirs inside of me.

Seriously, what the hell were these feelings?

I'm brought back to reality when I hear the voice of the cruelest man I've ever met.

"How was your service?" Li Wei.

Chen chuckles at his father's question. "The service was excellent. Just what I needed. I'll definitely have her service me again."

Asshole.

Although I knew he was putting on an act for his father, hearing him say things like that made me want to grab his balls and twist them.

"Do you think she makes a good whore?"

My heart pounds as I wait for Chen's answer.

"I think she makes an excellent whore, father. It was the right decision in bringing her here."

Prick.

"It was, but she's still far from obedient. Even after killing her father, I hear that she's still acting like a wild animal." Li Wei's tone was sharp.

The mention of my father made the nausea swirl unrestrained in my empty stomach. Up until now, I had tried so hard to block it out because I wanted to focus more on getting out of here with a clear head, but it seems like everyone here is out to get me. Always reminding me of what I've already lost and what I will also lose if I try to escape again.

*Eomma...***(Mom)**

"Every animal can be tamed, father." Chen assures.

Not me.

I hear Li Wei sigh. "Not this one."

Was that fear I heard in his voice?

"Maybe after a few punishments from me, that might change." I hear the smile in his voice and tense my jaw.

"How do you expect me to believe that?" Li Wei asks coldly. "Not even Yuta could tame her. What makes you think you can succeed?"

"*Duìbùqǐ.*" Chen mutters. **(I'm sorry)**

There's a long pause and then I hear footsteps advancing towards me. I watch Li Wei pass and stand up just in time for me to bump into Chen.

"You think I make a good whore, do you?" I spat.

Chen rolled his eyes. "What did you want me to say? That you sucked? Saying that will no doubt get you punished and I don't want that."

I look around the area and hide my disgust when I see that most of the customers were either drunk out of their asses or their tongues were halfway down someone's throat.

"I think I'd rather take the punishment than be here right now." I say gruffly.

Chen takes a step closer to me. "Lower your voice. You never know who might be listening."

I wave around the area. "Like who? Everyone's too busy participating in sexual acts."

Chen leans down to my ear. "Need I remind you that we're not meant to speak casually like this when we're in the company of my father and my brothers? We can't make them suspicious. But continue behaving like this, and neither of us will get out of here alive."

Before I can open my mouth, he moves past me and sits at a table in the far end of the room, accompanied by his father and Kang. As Chen approaches, Kang shoves one of the whores away from him and offers Chen the seat next to him. Immediately after Chen sits, Kang pours his brother a drink with a cheerful smile. I peek a glance over at the table, to see Ling already making her way over to their table. The huge parasol blocks my vision of where she's chosen to sit, but something tells me that she was near Chen. Looking at recent events, her behavior from this morning suddenly makes sense. She liked him.

I wanted to smile and be happy for her, but the corners of my mouth refused to comply.

The image of her sitting on his lap fabricated inside my head and the next thing I know, I'm suddenly filled with rage. When did my hands turn into fists? When did my brows furrow?

An acidic feeling slices at me.

Was this jealousy?

I move my head over and snarl when I see that she's indeed placed herself on Chen's lap. I take a step forward, not knowing what my true intentions are when an arm snakes around my waist, pulling me back into a solid chest. I gasp in surprise when I feel the stranger's five o'clock shadow brushing against my jaw.

"Looking for me?"

My eyes widen at the familiar voice.

I swing my head back over to the table and glance at every single face that was in attendance, but one familiar face was missing.

Yuta's.

My breathing increases as it dawns on me who's standing behind me. "Yuta?"

"Were you looking for me?" He says seductively.

I turned in his arms and took a step back. "What makes you think I'd be looking for you? You're not exactly an oil painting."

He clutched his heart. "You wound me."

I looked down at his hands and spat. "You don't even have a heart. Or if you do, it's completely dead inside."

He glares in disapproval through his strands of hair then turns me again in his arms, his protruding length pressing against my backside. He brings up his other hand, placing it around my neck and turns it in Chen's direction. "And Chen? Is his heart also dead inside?"

I watch as Ling places her hand against Chen's chest,

leans down to his ear, and mouths something that makes him laugh. I avert my eyes and stare down at the floor. "*Méiyǒu.* **(No)** He's less of a monster than you."

His hand trails up my thigh. "Is that what you think? Have you forgotten that he's a Jinyoung?"

My chest rises and falls rapidly. "He's nothing like you or Kang. He might be a Jinyoung, but at least with him, I don't need to pretend to enjoy his company."

Yuta pulled me harder against him. My eyes rolled back at the feeling. "So, you're saying that all of the times we've fucked, you've not enjoyed it?"

No comment.

I tried to move my head to look at him, but because of his strength, it was a losing battle. My upper body couldn't move an inch. He keeps my head pinned in Chen's direction and whispers in my ear. "Have you fucked him? You probably have considered he can't keep his eyes off you. Tell me, is he a good fuck? Does he fuck better than me? Did he make you come?"

My eyes fluttered open as I cleared my throat. "Just because you're somewhat of a good lay, doesn't make you any less a decent person."

He places his hot mouth against my neck, causing me to gasp in surprise. Yuta takes hold of my wrists and pins them behind my back, consuming the skin on my shoulder, nipping my collarbone, running his warm tongue down the trail of my jaw. My eyes rolled back and the moment they focused again, they met Chen's.

My eyes widened in panic.

The intensity in his eyes was unlike anything I'd ever seen. He looked at me, then down at Yuta's hand around my waist, then tensed his jaw.

My feelings were all over the fucking place.

I twirl around, giving Yuta a hateful glare and shove his chest. Ignoring my gaze, Yuta looks in the direction behind me and grins. "You two make it so fucking obvious."

I could only stare at him and gape.

"He's not here to reminisce, is he?" Yuta asks as he puts his hands in his pockets.

Nope.

"Why ask something you already know? You knew he'd never forgive you for what you did to his mother, so why bother ask such a fucking dumb question?"

"Watch your mouth." Yuta's hand shot out and gripped my jaw. "Remember who you're talking to."

I chuckle to myself.

Just like when somebody told me to do something, it

went in one ear and out the other.

As soon as his grip lessened, I removed his hold on me and grinned. “Seriously, do you really think he wants to patch things up with you? He doesn’t.”

A pause.

He studies me with a smirk. “You think you’re so smart, don’t you?”

“Doesn’t matter what I think. All I can think about now is getting out of here and getting away from you.”

“*Shénme*?” **(What?)** Yuta asked.

Ignoring his question, I looked up towards the clear blue sky and smiled. “My time here is almost over.”

Yuta frowns. “*Nǐ zài shuō shénme*?” **(What are you saying?)**

I square my shoulders and thrust out my chin. “I’m saying that soon, I’ll be free.”

I just had to be patient until then.

He runs his hand through his hair. “We’ve already talked about this. You’re never getting out of here, sweetheart.”

Wrong.

I nod. “Yes, I am.”

Another pause.

"I didn't want to say this but, you do remember the reason why your father died, right?"

My heart sank.

Yuta pointed at me. "He died because of you."

Fuck you.

I gasp as my bottom lip trembles. "Shut up."

"Have you forgotten about that? Or maybe you don't give a shit about him because you only care about yourself."

"I said shut up." I snarled.

But he continues on.

"Did you also forget whose life is on the line if you escape? You wouldn't want your mother to end up like your father, would you?" Yuta says amusingly.

I clench my fists as my breathing increases. He could probably tell I was close to exploding because he changes his demeanour instantly.

"*Josimhae*, **(Be careful)** my father's watching." Yuta murmured. "We wouldn't want him to find out the real reason why Chen's back, would we?"

I shrugged. "Go ahead and tell him. You'd be helping me out a lot actually."

"Oh really? How?"

"Things are going a little too slow for my liking. Telling him might speed things up."

He takes my hand and leads me towards the table where his brothers are sitting. Li Wei was nowhere to be seen. Also sitting at the table were some of Li Wei's regular guests, smoking cigarettes and cigars. I couldn't help but notice some of them had even brought their own whores with them.

Poor souls.

Yuta sits in the chair opposite to Chen's and places me on his lap. He takes out a cigarette, lights it and takes a drag, then looks away from me as he blows the plume of smoke to the side.

"Tell me, Ling. Has Chen fucked you yet?" Kang winks at her while pouring himself another drink.

She glances over at me to see if I'm watching, then kisses Chen's cheek. "Not yet, sir. But one can only hope."

It will happen in your dreams.

Chen holds the cigarette between his thumb and middle finger with a far-away look in his eyes.

Kang leans forward. "*Come on, gàosù wǒ.*" **(Tell me)**

She smiled shyly.

Pathetic.

"Is who I fuck any business of yours, brother?" Chen glares at his younger brother. He wraps his lips around the filter, causing a tingle between my legs.

"But Chen, when will you fuck her?" Kang asks. "She's liked you for fucking ages and yet you still haven't tasted that sweet tight pussy of hers..."

"Maybe I have fucked her?" Chen says nonchalantly.

Behind me, Yuta scoffed.

My eyes shoot across the table. "Have you?"

And just like that, all conversation around the table came to a stop and everyone's eyes were on me.

Shit!

I had spoken out of turn.

I lower my head. "*Duìbùqǐ.*" **(I'm sorry)**

Yuta wraps a hand around my neck and squeezes. "*Nǐ xiǎng shòudào chéngfá ma*?" **(Do you want to be punished?)**

Punishment was the last thing I wanted.

I shook my head. "No, sir."

He releases my neck and sighs in disappointment. "What a shame. I was hoping you'd say yes to the punishment."

Kang chuckled. "You know, not everyone wants to

spend time with you, brother."

"Says the one who's sitting right next to me." Yuta barks.

Ignoring his brothers, Chen leans forward and eyes me. "What I do in my own personal time isn't any of your business, whore."

Ouch.

His words stung my eyes.

I lower my eyes, hurt by his cruel and savage act.

"Is that understood?" Chen utters.

The next time we'll be alone, he'd better prepare himself for a slap.

I nod. "*Shì de xiānshēng.*" **(Yes, sir)**

Kang guffaws. "Spending some time in the states has turned you into a fucking savage, brother."

Savage indeed.

Not wanting to spend time in either of their companies any longer, I remove myself from Yuta's lap and bow to the table. "Excuse me for a moment."

But with a firm grip to my hip, he pulls me back down on him, leaning into my ear. "*Nǐ rènwéi nǐ yào qù nǎlǐ*?" **(Where are you going?)**

I turn my head and lower my voice. "To the

bathroom? *Wae*? **(Why?)** Is it prohibited?"

He grins. "You're not going to cry because he snapped at you, are you? If you are, then do it here because nothing gives me more pleasure than seeing a girl cry. It gives me such a hard-on."

What a sick bastard.

"I'll never give you the satisfaction of seeing me cry again." I stand up for the second time and excuse myself. "Excuse me."

After leaving the table, I take a couple of steps but then look back to see that Ling's removed herself from Chen's lap and is now standing between his legs. Nauseating jealousy rises up and chokes me. One of her perfectly manicured hands was placed around his shoulder while the other trailed up and down his chest. I watch as Chen moves her hair over her shoulder and smiles flirtatiously at her.

Bitch.

In the corner of my eye, I see one of the servers who's delivered our drinks throughout the day coming back towards our table, carrying a tray full of drinks. I take a couple of subtle steps backward, nearing back towards Chen's table and place my foot out just in time for the server to pass me. And just as I had hoped, the server trips over my foot and spills the complete tray of drinks all over Chen and Ling. Gasps and grunts come from around the table at the unexpected scene that's occurred before them. Before anyone can suspect me, I walk away as though nothing's happened when suddenly someone grabs a handful of my hair and yanks my head upwards.

Li Wei.

Shit!

Everyone crammed into the space to witness the spectacle I'd caused. Li Wei stares at me in absolute hatred for a few seconds, then without a word, he steps forward and smacks me across the face. I gasp as scorching pain reverberated from my cheek and throughout my body.

Li Wei's voice was calm. "I'm not sure what you were thinking, but this is the most profound disobedience to me yet. You will be punished for your actions."

I nod.

"I thought you had learned your lesson after what happened to your father, but obviously not."

I swallow hard and sneak a glance over at Chen. I didn't want to look at him, couldn't face the guilt of what I'd done. At first, his face was shocked but it quickly changed to concern. He stands from his chair, practically shoving a soaking wet Ling off to the side and comes to stand next to Yuta.

Li Wei releases my hair and waves me off. "One of you, get her out of my sight and punish her. And someone clean up this fucking mess!"

The server who I'd tripped gave me a confused look then got on her knees and began cleaning the mess I'd caused.

Ashamed, I looked over at the brothers and noticed that Yuta's eyes were hungry. He reaches out and grabs my wrist when a voice halts his movements.

"*Děngdài.*" **(Wait)**

Li Wei.

The room quietens as every set of eyes turn towards Li Wei as he addresses his sons. "Chen is to punish her."

Yuta frowned. "*Shénme*?" **(What?)**

Chen stepped forward and grabbe the wrist Yuta's holding with a smirk on his face. "I am to conduct the punishment this time, brother. So please, step aside."

Chapter 15

Chen

I stared at my brother and waited patiently for him to respond. I knew he was angry. Furious that I'd overstepped, but sadly for him, I wasn't going to allow either Kang or Yuta punish Maggie anymore. No, their time with her was over.

"*Nǐ juédé nǐ zài zuò shénme*?" **(What do you think you're doing?)** Yuta growled.

My lips quirked up in a sly smirk. "What does it look like I'm doing, brother? I'm obeying father's orders."

I was prepared to fight if it would come to that but knowing Yuta, he wouldn't want to cause a scene. Not in front of the guests and certainly not in front of our father. If there was one thing I knew that Yuta hated it was disappointing our father. And so, without another word, Yuta stared coldly at me and stepped aside.

"Let her go." I motioned to his hand still wrapped around Maggie's wrist.

"You're making a huge mistake." Yuta muttered as he released her.

Ignoring his threat, I pushed Maggie behind me and politely thanked him. "*Xièxiè*." **(Thank you)**

But just before I passed my brother, Yuta reached out and leant into my ear. "Don't ever humiliate me like that again."

"Or what?" I asked amusingly.

Yuta's face darkened as he shouldered past me. "Do it again, and you'll find out."

The minute he was out of sight, all the tension inside my body deflated, only for it to return when I realised what the hell I'd gotten myself into.

With Maggie's wrist in my grasp, we made our exit and walked in silence down the halls, making our way into the punishment room. Even alone, I still couldn't bring myself to look at her. Still couldn't understand why she did such a thing with many prying eyes watching her. I had seen the way the server had looked at Maggie and knew she didn't have anything to do with the whole incident. But why cause a scene like that? To get herself into trouble? Why would Maggie do something like that?

I had been keeping an eye on Maggie, and immediately noticed the change in her behaviour when Ling had approached me. She'd spoken to me about the old times. Both good and bad. But then the next thing I know, a tray full of drinks land on myself and Ling. At first, I thought it might've been an accident; that the server perhaps lost her footing, but I couldn't shake off the look Maggie had on her face before turning away. It looked almost sinister-like.

I opened the solid double doors to a dim-lighted room. I stepped inside and shuddered. Now, I was no prude, but this room scared the shit out of me. Repulsed me even.

Without looking at me, Maggie timidly followed me inside the room. I closed the doors behind her and brushed my hands over the canes, whips, and floggers adorning the wall "This is the first time I've stepped foot in here."

Maggie remained silent as she stood in the centre of the room, her shoulders slumped, her eyes downcast, just as she'd been taught.

I shook my head and scoffed. "You've been in this room before, I gather?"

"Why have you brought me here?" She asked.

I shrugged nonchalantly. "To punish you. Why else?"

She cocked her head to the side and frowned. "Tell me you're joking."

"Eyes down!" I roared.

She gasped in shock at my outburst which immediately turned into a glare. Maggie looked far from happy.

Pause.

"Why are you doing this?"

I pursed my lips, looked to the side, and stayed silent for a few moments.

"Chen!?" She shrieked.

I arched a brow. "Ten strikes should be enough, right?"

"What are you doing?"

I sighed. "What I'm supposed to do. Punish you."

Not only was I here to punish her, but I was also curious to know why she tripped up the server. I didn't want to punish her. Hell, I'd never lay a hand on her, but I had no choice. We were being watched.

"Tell me, why did you do it?" I asked as I rummage through different drawers in the room until I come across some rope.

Maggie's body tenses at my question.

"Why did you do it?" I repeated as I grabbed her hands and tied her wrists together.

She grimaced at my roughness and she asked. "Do what?"

Motioning her to the centre of the room, I discarded my waistcoat and shirt. "Why did you trip up the server, making her spill the drinks all over Ling and myself?" I slowly lowered her to her knees, and from where I was standing, I had a perfect view of her from behind, my eyes immediately going straight to her rounded ass.

I slowly walked around her and propped one hip on the side of the gargantuan bed and looked down at her. “Why did you do it?"

"I don't know what you're talking about." She spat.

I knew what she was doing. Know she was putting on an act to hide the truth, but what she doesn’t know is that I saw everything.

I slyly grinned. “Because I saw you. You tripped her up with your own foot. Am I wrong?”

Without a word, she turned her head and faced me. "I didn’t like what I saw, okay?”

I hid my grin as she becomes flustered. "I can't exactly explain what I'm feeling right now but..."

“Come here.” I ordered.

My heart pounded as she stood up and walked towards me. She kept her eyes locked on mine, but her face was completely void of emotion.

I gently cupped her cheek and planted a kiss on her forehead. and motioned with my chin to the arm bench, placed at the end of the bed. “Bend over.”

Maggie’s breathing was all ragged as she climbed over the bench, placing her bound hands in front of her while lowering her stomach on top of it. I place my hand on her lower back and close my eyes when I hear her suck in a breath. She squirms and struggles. I knew she didn't like to be restrained, but there wasn't any other way of doing this. This was a punishment. A punishment she'd brought down upon herself.

I respond to her squirming by slapping her ass hard. She gasps and squirms even more. I spank her again and pin her down onto the bench.

One.

With my hand, I circle the soft, creamy skin of her ass, then raise the same hand and bring it down with a loud smack.

Two.

Maggie tenses again. My third slap lands in the exact same spot.

Three.

"*Gwaenchanh-a*?" I asked. **(Are you okay?)**

She growled in response. "Fuck you."

I spank her again, harder than before.

Four.

Maggie squirms and tries to close her legs, but I use my hand to separate them apart. I grab her hair and pull her head back. "Five more to go."

Maggie rasps as she clenches her eyes shut. Her forehead creases in discomfort, but she remains silent.

When the fifth smack sounded, she let out her first whimper. Without a doubt, I knew it must've hurt because even my own hand was beginning to sting. The skin on her arse had begun to redden in response to each of my strikes.

Five.

Not wanting to prolong this punishment even longer, I carry out the final five smacks one after the other without pause. After the tenth slap, she lets out a pained moan then arches her back in need.

Was she turned on right now?

I take a step back and rip the material she wears around her hips, then place my hand between her legs to find her entrance wet.

Did my spankings do this to her? I smile to myself at the thought.

My fingers glided in and out of her pussy, stroking her channel and her entrance and her clit. Her wetness smeared everywhere, even running down her thighs.

I shove two fingers deep inside of her, making her moan. I could feel that she was far wetter on the inside than on the outside. I unzip my pants and take my cock out. Maggie moans as she feels the head of it rubbing against her slit. With a grin, I alternate by teasing her entrance and her clit with the head and fingering her with two of my fingers.

I smirk even though she can't see my face. "How are you finding my punishment so far?"

She remains silent.

"Maggie?"

Again, she says nothing.

"Do you perhaps want this?" I tease while rubbing my cock against her. "Is that what you want?"

Maggie turns her head against the arm bench and glared up at me.

I take my position and rub my shaft against her entrance. "I asked you a question, Mags. Answer me."

"Fuck you, Chen." She rasps.

"Do you want my cock inside of you?" I ask light – heartedly. "Do you want to be fucked?"

I knew she wanted it, could see her need clearly, but she forces herself to shake her head. I grab a fistful of her hair again and lean down, my weight atop her, pinning her body firmly to the bench.

Tucking myself away, I release her bound hands and whispered in her ear. "This is a punishment sweetheart, not a fuck."

Shoving herself away from me, she shoulders past me and headed for the exit. "I fucking hate you."

Grabbing her wrist, I bring her to face me. “I only did what I had to do.”

“We wouldn’t even be in this position right now if we’d made our escape a lot sooner.”

I closed my eyes, exhaled and met her eyes. “In the future, try not to get caught tripping up servers and all will be well.”

"Don't blame this on me!"

“I told you. I’m waiting for the right moment.”

She growled in frustration. “And when will that be exactly?”

I shrugged. “*Wǒ bù zhīdào.* **(I don’t know)** The perfect opportunity hasn’t presented itself yet. Be patient.”

“I’ve been nothing but patient!” Maggie shrieked.

“Maggie...”

“No!” She spat. “When you came here, you were adamant on getting us both out of here, and yet we’ve not made a single move. What changed?”

Suddenly, the door opens to reveal my father causing my heart to jolt. He had a very satisfied smirk on his face as approaches the two of us.

Both Maggie and I bowed in greeting.

Without looking at me, he palms Maggie's backside and leans down to her ear. "Did you behave yourself?"

She raises her head and stares into my eyes while answering. "Yes, sir."

"Are you in any pain?" Li Wei asked.

Again, her eyes remain glued to mine.

"Yes, sir." She repeated.

"And have you learned your lesson?"

"Yes, sir."

He chuckled in response. "Good."

Li Wei turns her roughly to face him and shoves one of his hands deep into her hair and fists it, forcing her face up to his. "Don't ever do something like that again. Understand?"

"Yes, sir." Maggie breathed as she bowed.

"Did you find the reason why she behaved so recklessly, Chen?" Li Wei asked.

I rack my brain to come up with something other than the truth because the last thing I want is to cause Maggie any more pain. But it's a struggle.

I come up with the only thing I could think of and cleared my throat. "It was purely a misunderstanding, father. The server did in fact trip over her own feet and misled us to believe that Maggie was the cause of the incident. You must fire that server at once."

I held my breath, waiting to see if he'd take the bait. And he does.

He tutted in disappointment. "Where do I get these pathetic and incompetent servers from? She must be dealt with accordingly."

Duìbùqǐ, **(I'm sorry)** fellow server, but I had to keep Maggie safe.

I bowed my head. "I shall get rid of her right away, sir."

My father nodded. "*Shì*, **(Yes)** you must."

I bowed to leave only for him to study me in a way that halted my movements. He looked at me in confusion then motions to Maggie. "Wait a minute. You still punished her even though she was innocent?"

"*Shì.*" **(Yes)**

"Why?" He ordered.

"I wanted to punish her. I figured this kind of opportunity might not come up again so I took advantage of the situation. I apologize if I have offended you father." I lied.

With a nod of approval, Li Wei turned back to Maggie, then kissed her on the forehead. "Maybe there is hope for you after all."

I see her clench her fists but say nothing. I knew she wouldn't do anything to my father because she wasn't stupid.

"I know that it must be hard for you considering you've just lost your father, but that doesn't mean you can do what you wish. Stop acting like a petulant child and accept your fate to what it is."

Maggie would never accept this life.

Li Wei continued. "Everything you do in this house has its consequences, and even though it doesn't feel like it, somebody's always watching you. You are never truly alone."

"Yes, sir." Maggie uttered.

"Nothing gets past me. Nothing."

I frowned as I listened to his words. Did he not believe me about the whole server situation? Did he know something that I didn't?

Have I been made to look like a fool? I shuddered at the thought.

"Don't ever let your emotions get in the way of the rules and of your role here, otherwise, your mother will meet the same fate as your late pathetic father."

Maggie's eyes wandered, but she bowed nevertheless. "Yes, sir."

Although he was my father, I still hated him. Hated him for being the manipulative bastard that he was.

"Leave and retire for the evening." Li Wei ordered .

Maggie bowed again. "Yes, sir."

With one final look at me, she leaves without a word, closing the door gently behind her. Now alone, Li Wei walks to the double French glass doors, opens them and stands on the balcony gazing out at the ocean.

"How did the punishment go, my son?" He asked while lighting a cigarette. "Did you enjoy yourself?"

I meet him on the balcony and placed my hands behind my back. "Did you not watch it on the monitors, father? Could you not see the pleasurable look I had on my face?"

He chuckled. "*Shì*, **(Yes)** that I did."

It sickened me to think that he'd been watching me.

"It went well, father. I hope I did not disappoint you." I say while trying not to grit my teeth.

He takes a drag from the cigarette. "That you did not. You seemed to enjoy yourself very much."

I had enjoyed myself, but only because I was spending time with Maggie.

I faked a smile. "I did. Never in my life have I experienced such pleasure. I cannot wait to do it again."

My father smiled. "Good. Very good. Being that you're back here for good, there'll be plenty of whores you can punish."

I looked out at the sea to see that a single boat was docked in the harbor. It probably belonged to one of my father's guests. Looking at it gave me ideas on how to get myself and Maggie out of here.

"Tell me father, whose boat is that?" I pointed to the docked boat.

Li Wei looked at the boat I'm pointing at then nods to it. "A beauty, isn't she? That boat there belongs to Sal. It was one of the gifts I bought for his birthday."

"Sal's here?"

Li Wei nodded. "These days, he's taken a particular interest in Shuang. I even heard that he wishes to purchase her for himself."

Kang won't be pleased...

"How long has he been at the villa?"

Father thinks for a moment. "About a week. And it doesn't look like he's leaving anytime soon."

Suddenly, an idea begins to form in my head.

"Then, he won't mind if we borrow it?"

"For what reason?"

I faked a smile. "Don't you remember how you used to take myself and my brothers out onto the ocean and taught us how to ride a speedboat when we were younger?"

He studied me carefully. "*Dāngrán.*" **(Of course)**

"Let us do that again. Not the speedboat part of course. We already know how to do that, thanks to you, father."

A tense pause.

His brow rises. "So, you wish to go out to sea?"

I nod. "Yes, sir. Just like old times."

"Why all of a sudden?"

I shrugged. "We have not spent much time together with just the four of us, and I miss it. Put aside your business meetings for one day and spend it with your beloved sons instead."

What I needed was to get my father alone, away from all the guards and then make my move.

And as for my brothers? I hadn't thought that far ahead yet.

My pulse was going into overdrive as I waited patiently for his response, but then a small smile lifted the edges of my father's mouth. "Early tomorrow morning, myself and your brothers will go out onto the yacht and bathe in the morning sun. Just like old times."

Hook, line, and sinker.

I smiled brightly. "I look forward to it."

Li Wei answered by giving me a creepy smirk.

I excused my father with a bow headed straight to my room. When I reached it, I got right to it and thought of possible ideas to stop my father. When tomorrow comes, I want my plan to be perfect. Every single detail must be thought out carefully. There was no room for mistakes. Especially not tomorrow because I was planning on making my move.

Tomorrow, I was getting both Maggie and myself the fuck out of here.

With an exhale, I make a phone call.

Chapter 16

Chen

Early the next morning, I found Yuta already waiting outside my bedroom door. It was a beautiful, bright morning, perfect for fishing and an assassination attempt.

With a gun strapped to my back, I dressed in a pair of shorts and a plain vest, slid on my sunglasses and walked beside my brother in silence down to the docks.

"Kang not coming?" I asked casually.

"Apparently so." Yuta replied in a bored tone.

Good.

That was one less brother to deal with.

Yuta continued. "A server did knock on his door, but Kang chose not to answer."

"Is that so? That's disappointing." I lied.

Yuta removed his sunglasses and placed them neatly on his head. "No bother. I'm here instead to keep an eye on you."

I frowned. "Keep an eye on me? Why would you need

to do that?"

"Because God knows what you're up to."

He shouldered past me, leaving me to wonder wether I should continue on with my plan, but another opportunity might never arise again. I had to try...for Maggie's sake.

Li Wei was already waiting. He was sitting on a barstool in the outside bar with a girl standing behind him. My heart galloped when I saw the figure with blue hair. My eyes immediately zero in on Maggie who was wearing a white bikini and a black oversized sun hat.

Approaching my father, I bowed, sat next to him and stared lovingly at the breakfast spread in front of me. "

"Whiskey?" Li Wei asked.

At this hour? Absolutely not.

I grimaced. "No, thank you. Just an orange juice for me."

My father clicked his fingers and immediately a server came and poured me a glass. I pay the server no notice and instead glance over at Maggie who had her head still bowed towards the floor. I couldn't see her eyes, but what I could see was her mouth. The corners were lifted upwards. Was she happy I was here? The thought made my chest swell.

My father brings up his hand and smacks Maggie on the backside, bringing me out of my trance. "I thought I'd bring Maggie here to tag along with us this morning. Hope you don't mind?"

Although I was thrilled to see her, I couldn't help but think that it wasn't just a coincidence that she was here. Something wasn't right.

"Of course, it is." I cleared my throat. "But if I may ask, what happened to having just the four of us?"

Li Wei looked around. "I don't see Kang here, do you?"

"He's probably busy fucking one of the whores." Yuta uttered.

I smirked. "Or several."

"Problem solved!" Li Wei chuckled and slapped Maggie's backside again. "The girl can take your brother's place."

The boat pushed away from the docks, moving at a pleasant speed and off we went out towards the glimmering blue-green sea. I excuse myself from the bar, giving the excuse of wanting a better view of the sea. From what I could tell, nobody cared about my excuse. Li Wei spares me no glance and waves me off, dismissing me.

As I moved away from the bar and back towards the

rear end of the yacht, I took in every single detail around me. As far as I could see, there were only two of my father's bodyguards on the boat. Biting lip, I noticed they were the bodyguards Li Wei took everywhere with him. They were like his very own hounds. He moved, they moved. I wouldn't be surprised if he made them wait outside the bathroom door while he took a shit. Hell, they probably wiped his ass for him.

Yuta stood to the side with his arms crossed, also looking out towards the sea. There was also the captain driving the boat, but he won't be a problem. As soon as the guns start to go off, he'll jump overboard and get the hell out of here. That is if he has a brain. I keep an eye out for more people but for now, it was only the eight of us.

Earlier back at the bar, my father didn't appear to be armed, but I knew his bodyguards were. They were heavily armed.

Suddenly, my back tingled, letting me know that somebody was approaching me. I continued facing forward and waited for the person to speak.

"You're nervous." A quiet feminine voice came from beside me.

It wasn't a question. It was a statement.

"Is it that obvious?" I asked, not looking at her.

I see Maggie nod her head in my peripheral vision. "Yes, but what I don't understand is why."

I slowly turned my head and looked at her with sincerity. "Today's the day."

Both of her brows rise. "What?"

I looked around warily, ignoring the curious glances Yuta made in our direction. "I'm making my move. Today."

A pause.

She looked down at herself and took in her appearance. "Well, you sure picked a fine day to pick a fight, Chen."

My lips quirked at the sides remembering her punishment la yesterday. "How's your ass today?"

She glared at me. "When will you make your move."

I wave off the question. "Never mind that. Just hide somewhere until I come and get you."

"Hide? I'm not a coward!" She whisper-yelled. "How many men have we got?"

With a heavy exhale, I looked out towards the sea. "Seven. Including us."

"Should be easy enough." Maggie says confidently. "

I scoffed. "It would be if one particular person wasn't here."

Yuta.

She's biting her lip with a faraway look in her eyes. "We've gone through a lot worse before. We'll be fine."

I wasn't entirely convinced.

"You think he's armed?" She asked hesitantly.

I nodded. "Without a doubt. Yuta goes nowhere without his gun. I'll even bet that he's got at least two guns on him right now."

There was a long silence until she spoke again.

"Fuck, how are we going to do this?" Maggie asked

I shrugged. "*Nado molla.*" **(I do not know)**

Silence.

Her jaw dropped. "You don't have a plan?"

I met her eyes. "If I did, I definitely wouldn't tell you about it."

She looked off to the side, spotted the emergency ax hanging in the glass compartment and smirked. "Fine. You've got your plan and I've got mine."

My eyes widened in alarm. "Don't do anything stupid, Maggie. Not today."

She leant closer to me. "If there's one person who's going to fuck this up, it's going to be you. And I swear to god, if we don't get through this today, I'm blaming you."

I watched as she leaves my side and headed back towards my father, who was now accompanied by my brother. I watched as she approached them, and tensed my jaw when I see Yuta pulling her down onto his lap, fisting her hair. What bothered me was the fact that she didn't look the least bit uncomfortable sitting there. Maybe it was part of her act, I don't know, but it bothered me. A lot.

Looking back, I didn't know that it would come to this. All those weeks ago back in America when we'd first captured Maggie, I didn't think my feelings for her would grow as strong. I wasn't the type to fall in love easily, but I loved her so much it hurt.

I remember her father approaching me all that time ago, and asked me to look out for his daughter for him while he wasn't around. At first, it was a nuisance because who in their right mind would want to look out for a moody hormonal teenage girl? Not me. But as time passed, my feelings for her began to change.

Back then, the mere sight of her annoyed me, but seeing her now, filled my body with desire. I wanted her. Wanted her every single day for the rest of my life and make her happy. That much was true. I'd never felt like this for a woman before and I sure as hell wasn't going to let it go. She's one in a million.

Taking one long look back at the sea, I turned and joined them in the lounging area and before I sat on the vacant chair, I bowed to my father who was watching my every move. Li Wei rested his hands behind his head and leant back, eyeing me curiously.

"Feeling a little seasick, are we?"

I placed my hand against my abdomen. "A little, yes. I think I drank too much last night."

I looked over to see Yuta eyeing me, as though he had something to say. I raised a brow, waiting patiently for him to open his smart mouth. And he does.

Yuta grinned. "Last night, you nagged father about wanting to reminisce about the old times by going fishing together, only for you show up off your face the next day. Could you be any more selfish, brother?"

I bowed my head towards my father. "Forgive me, father."

At this, Li Wei raised his brow.

Yuta continued, unfazed. "Why lie though? Because from what I recall, you didn't even drink last night."

I frowned at him. "How would you know?"

His grin gets wider, if that was even possible. "I had cameras installed in every one of the rooms, and last night, none of the servers came to your room to deliver alcohol. As far as I can recall, you were asleep well before noon."

With every second that passed, I was growing increasingly uncomfortable.

I watched my father as he steepled his fingers over his chest. I watched him nod in Yuta's direction, and he disappears.

Li Wei continued. "Plus, you don't get seasick. We've been on boats for as long as I can remember, and you never get sick. Only Kang does."

Silence.

"Why are you lying to me, son?" Li Wei asked calmly.

Even the air seemed to come to a still.

I scoffed to hide my nerves. "What? Are you watching me now?"

"When I said that I'd be watching you, I fucking meant it." Yuta growled.

I sat forward on the edge of my seat, and rested my elbows on my knees, my fingers linked together as I stare into my brother's evil eyes. "You're jumping to conclusions. You don't know shit."

"Maggie." Li Wei interrupts.

She removed herself from Yuta's lap and bows. "Yes, sir?"

Li Wei points to the bar. "Would you be a dear and

grab me a bottle of whiskey."

She looked at me with an expressionless look on her face. I ever so slightly nod to make her aware of the fact that shit's about to go down when she leaves.

She nods back to me and addresses my father.

"Yes, sir." Maggie bowed again and skittered away.

When she disappears from view, my father turns to me and sighs. "Is there anything you wish to tell me, Chen?"

My stomach dropped.

Keeping myself calm and collected, I asked. "*Shèmiǎn*?" **(What?)**

"Let's cut the bullshit, shall we? You don't plan on staying here, do you?"

My eyes cut to Yuta to see him looking back at me with an apprehensive look in his eyes. Why was he nervous?

I frowned. "Father?"

"Do you plan on taking Maggie with you also?"

Shit!

How did he know?

"Surely, this is all a misunderstanding." I said calmly.

My father chuckled. "I wonder how long you've been

planning this escape for. A week? A month?"

"*Nǐ zài shuō shénme*?" **(What are you talking about?)**

But he ignored me. "And I suppose you thought you were going to succeed?"

I remained silent.

"Father..." Yuta starts.

Li Wei cut him off. "That whore you saved came to my office yesterday with tears in her eyes and revealed everything. She revealed every little dirty thing you've done and the things you're planning to do, including escaping here with The Bull's daughter."

Ling.

My first initial thought was how she knew about my plan. Had she overheard a conversation of ours? If so, why would she tell my father? I mean, how could she do this to me? After everything I'd done for her, this is how she repays me?

"I cannot allow it, my son. I won't allow you to take Maggie away. People are still searching for her, and if she returns back to her home, she could be traced back to me and if that happens, I'll be locked away for a very long time."

I snarled. "Well, maybe that's where you belong, father. In prison, rotting away in a cell all alone, waiting for death to consume you."

"Chen." Yuta warned.

He threw his head back and laughed, then his whole attitude changed. His entire face becomes serious as he glares at me. "When were you going to tell me that you were The Bull's informant?"

My skin crawled from the way he was looking at me.

Never.

Suddenly, both of my father's bodyguards came into view and stood protectively behind him, their hands resting on their guns.

I eyed them both. "In truth, I was never going to tell you."

His brows rise. "*Méiyǒu*?" **(No?)**

"No." I said truthfully. "I was going to take it to my grave, but I guess the cat's out of the bag."

He took a sip of his whiskey. "Indeed it is."

I heard Yuta click his tongue, but I paid him no attention.

I sighed. "You know, it was a shame he died."

Li Wei frowned at that while Yuta eyed me warily.

"He was a good man."

Li Wei's face turned to rage as his voice rises. "He

was the enemy!"

I pointed at my father. "To you, yes. But not to me."

His eyes widened. "Have you forgotten what he did to your fucking mother!?"

My stomach drops at the mention of my mother, but I shut it off and face my father. "I have not, but in his defence, he didn't know who he was shooting at the time. He was only following orders."

"And you can forgive him for that, can you?" Li Wei spat.

A pause.

"Answer me!" He barked.

"I can't forgive a dead man." I muttered. "Well, saying that, you're alive and I've not forgiven you for the things you've done. You're rotten to the core."

Yuta cleared his throat. "*Chén, bì zuǐ...*" **(Shut up)**

"What did you fucking say to me, boy!?" Li Wei yelled. "I'm your father..."

I cut him off. "He was more of a father to me than you ever were. In the small amount of time I had with him, he treated me like his own son. He never laid a hand on me, never punished me or treated me like a dog. He was the perfect role model. So, can you honestly blame me for wanting out?"

Before my father can respond to my outburst, I see Yuta going for his gun in my peripheral vision only for him to collapse a second later onto the floor. I looked over in confusion to see Maggie holding the red, steel ax in her hand with a satisfied smirk on her face.

"That's going to hurt tomorrow." She says, looking down at Yuta's lying form with a satisfied smirk.

While everyone's distracted by Maggie's entrance, I launched myself from my chair and towards one of the bodyguards. Li Wei shouts and soon bullets start going off in every fucking direction.

I threw myself at the bodyguard and we both land onto the ground as more bullets blast the glass doors, sending shards flying all around us.

Before the guard can regain his footing, I turned him over onto his back, straddled him and began punching his face repeatedly.

A gun slides across the deck next to me, I take a quick glance to the other side to see Maggie looking over in my direction. She smiles when she sees me with the gun in my hands.

As I bring up my fist to strike the bodyguard, he jabs me in the abdomen, leans forward and head-buts me. I collapse to the side to see Maggie being dragged away by the other guard.

She struggles against him, but he's too strong. But out

of nowhere, she brings up her leg and performs a roundhouse kick to the head. She then shoves him against the wall, her hand around his neck, pulls out a kitchen knife and stabs him repeatedly in the gut. Blood splatters every-fucking-where.

That's one man down.

I bring my attention back to the guard who's still recovering from my strikes when more shots ring out with more glass shattering. With the gun still in my hand, I bring it up to the bodyguard's head and shoot three times. His blood spraying my face.

Two down.

Maggie comes running towards me, her body drenched in blood and her eyes wide. "Where the fuck are these shots coming from? Did your father bring a sniper with him?"

"No, they're coming from the villa." I responded, coming to my feet.

She glanced around. "The villa?"

I nodded in confirmation.

"But aren't we far out?"

"We turned back halfway through the journey."

She frowned. "We did?"

I nodded again. "Father probably wanted to turn the

boat around because he had a plan. No doubt if we go back to the villa now, his men are going to be there waiting to kill us both. This boat trip was just a diversion to get his men inside the villa while the two of us were out of it."

"Fucker." Maggie spat.

I remained silent because she literally took the words out of my mouth.

"Speaking of your father, where is he?"

We looked around and immediately spot him sneaking away quietly down the stairs to the lower deck. Maggie brings up her arm, aims and throws the knife towards my father, hitting him in the shoulder.

"Damn, I missed." Maggie growled in frustration.

Li Wei collapsed down the stairs to the ground, clutching his bloodied shoulder, while screaming in agony. He reaches down his body, possibly looking for a gun, but I pointed my gun and shot just beside his head, halting his movements. "Don't."

But he doesn't listen and reaches for his gun anyway, and shoots me in the shin. It stings like a motherfucker.

In anger, I shoot his leg three times causing him to throw back his head and grunt in pain.

"Put the gun down." I ordered.

Ignoring me, he brings down his head and glares at me. “How could you do this?” Li Wei whisper-hissed.

I pointed my gun at him, my finger calmly placed on the trigger. “If I didn’t make my move first, you would’ve killed me.” I say nonchalantly. “And considering you’re already on the way to your grave, I just simply sped up the process.”

“You bastard! How could you betray your own family?” He said through painted breaths.

A pause.

“Chen!” Li Wei grunts. “Fucking answer me!”

I sighed. “You know, before my mother died, I would’ve done anything for this family. I would’ve done anything without question, even if that meant killing innocent people. I would’ve gladly followed in your footsteps and maybe one day become the leader of the triads, but then my mother died, and that’s when I realized what kind of family I’d been born into. I’d never been able to live in peace because I’ll always be surrounded by enemies. Enemies that, to begin with.” I clear my throat as my finger tightens on the trigger. “That’s why I’ve got to end this.”

I had to kill him otherwise I’d never be able to live normally.

Li Wei smiled but his voice is weak. “You’ll never be free.”

I remained silent and continued to stare at my father in disgust.

"Killing me won't change a thing." He rasped.

I shrugged. "Maybe it won't, but at least there's one less vile person in the world."

Li Wei growled. "My men will hunt you down and kill you and that whore!"

I placed my gun between my father's eyes. "Let them come. We'll be waiting. And after that, I'm going to burn your entire empire to the fucking ground."

A pause.

"Any last words?" I asked.

He brings up his head and studies me. "Never in my life did I think my own blood would kill me."

I chuckle. "Well, we're not exactly a normal family, are we?"

"You're no son of mine." He says as he chucks his gun away from him. Then, he clutches his shoulder and waits.

"Was I ever your son?" I ask. "Because I don't think you ever saw either of us as your sons. The three of us were just pawns to you."

My father goes to say something, but his mouth suddenly fills with blood.

“Seems like the afterlife’s calling for you, father.” He looks straight at me, his face completely void of any emotion, and just as I go to pull the trigger, a voice suddenly stops me.

“Wait.”

Maggie.

I turned my head and asked. “What is it?”

“He’s mine.” Maggie murmured.

A pause.

“I want to kill him.”

“Are you sure?”

She nodded. “He killed my father. Of course, I’m sure.”

I take a step back as Maggie walks casually towards him while dragging the ax alongside her and comes to stand in front of Li Wei. She tilts her head to the side, her eyes cold and empty as she takes in my father’s weak form. “How are you feeling? Oh wait, I don’t fucking care.”

My father begins to yell obscenities at her, but all that comes out of his mouth is blood.

She crouches down, meeting Li Wei eye to eye. “I’ve been waiting for this moment. Been waiting for this day for a very long time."

"You're making a huge mistake!"

She backhands my father. “You’ve ruined my life by harming the people I love, and for that, I’ll spit on your grave for as long as I live.”

She moves into position, standing behind my father’s head when I notice a single tear running down her face.

Maggie sniffled. “This is for my dad, you lowlife murdering cunt.”

I watch as she raises the ax over her head and brings it swinging down towards my father’s neck.

Chapter 17

Maggie

I watched as Chen threw his father's body overboard in silence and looked up towards the sky. "Rest in peace, father."

I hear the splash of the ocean and turned my head to face Chen who was already coming towards me with a blank expression on his face. "You okay?"

This morning I had been beyond delighted when I was given the chance of going outside the villa's walls and out to sea. The warmth of the sun had felt wonderful on my skin, and for a second I had begun to think that I was on vacation, and not held against my will. But all of that came crashing down when I stole glances in Chen's direction. I knew just by looking at him that something wasn't right. Every so often, I'd look at him and he'd looked anxious and restless. Seeing him like that had made me begin to worry, and I was right to assume so...

I released a heavy exhale, then replied with a nod. "You?"

Chen looked out towards the ocean, his brows furrowed, deep in thought. "I thought I'd feel something, anything but... I feel nothing. Nothing at all."

I watched him closely, bombarded with thoughts and questions, but now wasn't the time. He'd watched me murder his father seconds ago.

I looked down at the ground, where Yuta still remained tied up and asked."When do you think he'll wake up?"

Chen bit his lip. "He'll come around soon, and when he does, he's going to be pissed.

"I'm not worried about Yuta." I uttered his name in distaste.

Chen responded by arching his brow in question.

I sighed. "When we get back to the villa, how are we going to face your father's men with just the two of us? Why don't we just sail in the opposite fucking direction and get the hell out of Hong Kong?"

Chen shook his head. "I'm not leaving this country until I bring my father's empire down."

I raised my voice to try and get through to him. "There could be an army of men waiting for us back there! We go back there and it's going to be one hell of a losing battle on our fucking side."

"No, we won't." He drummed his fingers on the handrail. "Because we're not going to be alone."

"What?" I asked.

"I called the cops last night. I made an anonymous phone call and informed them of your situation, and they were quick to get on board in rescuing you."

"What makes you so sure that they'll turn up?" I murmured.

Before he could respond, his phone begins to ring. He pulled it out of his trouser pocket, looked at the screen and smiled a small smile. "Hold that thought."

He cleared his throat and brought the phone to his ear. "Are you in position? Very good. How many men do you see?" Chen tutted. "Why so many? No, I'm not that far away now. Once you see the boat, begin shooting immediately. I have the girl with me, so prepare the plane. I wish to leave with the girl as soon as possible."

He ended the call and looked at me reassuringly. "We've got back up there already, so you don't need to worry."

But I was. I was worried that I was getting my hopes up for nothing. If all goes well when we get back, it means that I'll be free and it means that I'll be able to go home. Back to my mother.

For once, God have mercy.

Just as we get to port, I notice Yuta beginning to stir in

the ropes. I couldn't help but grimace at how tight the knots looked on him. Don't get me wrong, I didn't pity Yuta. Not even in the slightest. Not after the things he'd done to me and my family. He deserved everything that was coming to him. Whatever that may be...

He slowly opened his eyes and looked dazedly at me, "Maggie?"

I tilted my head to the side and plastered an annoyed expression on my face. "Why couldn't you stay out for just a little bit longer? I was beginning to enjoy the peace and quiet."

"What happened?" Yuta demanded as he glared at his bound wrists. "Why am I tied up?"

Ignoring his questions, I crouched down in front of him and pouted. "How's the head?"

I bet it hurt like a bitch.

"That was you?" He asked through gritted teeth.

"It felt good too."

His lips quirked in a slight smirk. "I should've known."

One side of his face was covered in blood thanks to me. I point towards his head. "Does it hurt? You've lost a lot of blood."

"Like you care?" He spat.

"I don't..." I replied.

He scoffed. "You're not even the slightest bit sorry, are you?"

I pursed my lips. "Consider it as somewhat of a payback for the things you've done to me."

Yuta looked down at his bound body and chuckled. "I killed your father and this is what I get? A tap on the wrist?"

I leant into his face and growled. "Shut your mouth."

He stared heatedly into my eyes, and then down at my lips, then bit his own. "What would I get for killing your mother, I wonder? A spanking?"

I squared my shoulders and cleared my throat. "I haven't really decided what I'm going to do with you yet, but keep talking and I'm sure I'll think of something...creative."

He studied me for a few seconds then looked at something behind me. "Why are you so quiet, brother? It's unlike you to be quiet for this long."

I turned my head to see Chen still looking out at the sea, a peaceful look on his face.

I brought my head back forward to Yuta looking around with a frown on his face. "Where is everyone?"

I kepy quiet, marvelling at the sight of a rare agitated Yuta.

His voice grew louder and harsher. “Where’s everyone? Where’s father?”

A pause

His face changes to complete and utter rage. “Chen!”

“What?” Chen replied, finally acknowledging his brother.

“Where’s father? What did you do?”

“He’s dead.” Chen uttered simply.

Yuta lowers his head and shakes it. “Now’s not the time for joking.”

“I’m not joking. I threw him into the sea myself. He’s long gone.”

Yuta growled. “Bullshit!”

Chen shrugged. “It’s the truth.”

An evil glint appeared in Yuta’s eyes as his brow furrows. “Who killed him? Who the fuck killed my father!?”

Silence.

“That would be me.” I answered.

His head snapped in my direction. “You!? Why!?”

I smiled after a long pause. “Tit for tat.”

I hear Chen sigh behind me. “Release him. I can’t bear

the sight of my brother defenceless. Looking at him like this makes me pity him a little."

"I don't need your pity." Yuta spat.

As I started to undo the ropes, he sprang forward and wrapped one of his hands around my neck. "You killed him, did you? Answer me before I snap your neck like a fucking twig."

Ever so gently, I reach for the gun behind me and aimed it between his legs. "I wouldn't do that if I were you. I've got a gun aimed right at your cock and if I see you make even the slightest movement, I'll pull the trigger without any hesitation. So, I suggest you get the fuck off me if you want to keep both of your balls and still have the chance of having any offspring. And yeah, I killed him. Loved every second of it too and I'd gladly do it again."

We stared at each other and gasped when Yuta gently cupped my cheek. Suddenly, Chen comes out of nowhere, picks Yuta off of the ground and punched his brother in the face. "Back off."

Yuta stumbled backward, cursing and placed his hand at his jaw while staring at Chen in hatred. "Why did you kill him?"

Chen shrugged. "Think it's self-explanatory, don't you think?"

Yuta threw back his head and shook it repeatedly. "Do

you realize what you've done!? None of this would've happened if you had just waited."

Chen scowled at his older brother. "If I had a waited a couple more seconds, you would have shot me. Again."

Yuta marched until he stood nose to nose with his brother. "I was getting my gun to shoot the fucking bodyguards!"

Chen waved him off. "Bullshit!"

I watched and listened to the exchange between the brothers in amusement.

"You should be kissing my fucking ass right now, brother!" Yuta roars. "I saved your goddamn life!"

Chen's eyes widened. "You saved my life? Then, why did you sell me out to father?"

Yuta sighed in frustration. "I was baiting him to see if he knew anything, and he did! He knew everything because of that fucking whore you brought in! If I hadn't said anything, you'd be the one dead."

I rolled my eyes and stood between the two brothers. "You done? Because in case you might've forgotten, there's a shootout going on inside your villa. So, unless you want to find your other brother dead, I suggest you both shut the fuck up and tell the guy driving this boat to hurry up."

Both Yuta and Chen sized each other up.

"This isn't over, Yuta." Chen said.

"Oh, I'm counting on it, brother."

The three of us hurry off the boat and run up to the villa, where we can already hear gunshots. The boards of the dock moan under our weight as we rush towards the villa. Chen takes my hand, and interlocks our fingers together, holding me tight. I didn't think much of it. Chen probably didn't either considering how quickly he was walking.

My heart hammered in my chest as we arrived on the property. The front of the villa was completely deserted, other than a few dead bodies. I crouched down next to one of the bodies and grabbed anything that might be useful. I took the knives and the gun holstered at his chest, then peered up at the brothers. "This kill was recent."

I handed the gun to Chen who took it only to look at me in confusion. "Don't you want to keep the gun for yourself?"

I shook my head. "I never did like guns. I prefer knives. That way I can never miss my target."

The three of us enter inside the villa and split up. I enter the living area - the place dark and in complete disarray. Furniture had been toppled over, broken glass from the windows was shattered everywhere on the floor, and bullet holes decorated the walls.

I held my breath, but it was eerily quiet. I approached the door that led into the kitchen when an arm shoots out and tightly wraps around my waist. I grunted out and struggled, trying to angle the knife towards the attacker, but he roughly twists my wrist. Discomfort shots through my arm as the knife slipped through my fingers. I brought up my foot and collided it with the attacker's knee, resulting in me getting shoved into the coffee table and hitting my head on its corner. I black out for a split second as blood fills my mouth and trickles down onto my chin.

"*Qǐchuáng*!" **(Get up)** The attacker orders as his fingers twist into my hair and pulled me onto my feet. I growled out in frustration and demanded. "*Ràng wǒ zǒu*!" I demand. **(Let me go)**

But he didn't. He laughed and began to drag me into the kitchen by my hair when I saw Yuta fighting off a cop and one of Li Wei's men.

I frowned, thinking which side Yuta was on, when suddenly, I'm thrown to the ground in front of black slack, and when I look up, I saw a gun aimed right into my face.

"Where's Li Wei?" My attacker demanded.

I stared coldly back at him, resulting in me getting hit on the side of the head with the gun holder.

“Where’s Li Wei?” He asked again, harsher.

I ignored the blood running down the side of my head and chuckled. “Wouldn’t you like to know?”

At lightning speed, he brings back his foot and kicked me in the stomach. I toppled over and gasped for breath.

The attacker growled. “I will not ask you again.”

My attention was drawn away when I heard somebody breathing nearby. I looked over to my left to see a young looking cop staring at me in fright, He made gurgling noises while clutching his wounded abdomen. Just by looking at his wound, I knew he wouldn’t make it. In the next minute or so, he’d be dead.

At that moment, guilt was eating and pestering me. Poor guy probably woke up this morning and thought it would just be another day at the office. Being assigned to do a rescue mission probably didn’t even cross his mind. It depresses me that this is how it ends for him. In death.

I met the eyes of my attacker and scowl. “He’s dead. Li Wei’s dead.”

The attacker grabbed me by the hair and pulled me roughly against his chest, his hand wrapped tightly around my neck.

My eyes found the lying form of the young cop's and just like I had predicted, his body was lying completely motionless on the ground.

As I was led throughout the house, I was surrounded by the sound of fighting and gunfire when I see Yuta approaching, bloodied with a gun in each hand.

"Yuta?" The attacker shouted.

Yuta's face was a mask of fury as he glared at my capturer.

"She says Li Wei is dead. Is this true?" The attacker asked Yuta as he pressed the gun against my temple.

Yuta nodded. "*Shì*." **(Yes)**

I squirmed in the attacker's hold - trying to break free, but he was far too strong.

"*Shéi gàn de*!" **(Who did it?)**

Yuta shrugged as he motioned to me. "Ask her."

The attacker turned me in his arms, and just as he was about to strike me, he was thrust backward as a bullet ripped through his eye. His pained groans made me feel content, as I took this moment to grab the knife hidden inside my underwear and ram it into his gullet. Blood spluttered down his front as he slumped to the floor. Dead.

I heard Yuta clicking his tongue. "Why make him suffer more? He was practically dead after I shot him."

I swirled around and threw my knife at the wall in rage. “I had it under control!”

“Another second and you’d be dead.”

“Isn’t that what you want?” I asked through gritted teeth.

His face became serious as he pulled me against his chest. “If I wanted to kill you, I would have done it a long time ago.”

I stuttered as I pushed him away. “Where do you think Chen is?”

“He went to look for Kang.”

"Do you think he's alive." I asked as I retrieved the knife from the wall.

"Probably not."

I watched as Yuta reloaded his gun and frowned. “Whose side are you on?”

He peered at me with an expressionless look on his face as he shouldered past me. “Nobodies.”

Yuta and I made our way through the house, killing men who stood in our way until we reached a corridor with piles of dead bodies lying on the ground. My only guess was that Chen had already been here and was nearby.

Yuta pointed to the end of the corridor. “That’s Kang’s

room."

The two of us run to the end of the hall to see Kang's door wide open, and just as we go to enter the room, we see Chen coming out of it, his eyes red-rimmed.

I gasped. "Chen?"

No response.

I scanned down his body for any sign of injury. "Are you okay? Are you hurt?"

Still, nothing.

My frown deepened as I looked at him, unable to understand what had made him like this, until I looked around him to see an unmoving body lying on the ground.

I covered my mouth in shock.

"Kang's dead." Chen murmured.

I took a few steps forward into the room, only to be shoved aside by Yuta. I watched him as he took in the whole scene and dropped to his knees in front of his dead brother.

"How?" I asked only for it to be left unanswered.

"Kang?" Yuta said his brother's name softly.

Nothing.

With both of his hands, Yuta places them on Kang's

cheeks and moves his head side to side. “Kang, wake up!”

"Stop it! He’s dead, brother!” Chen cried. “We were too late, brother.”

“Be quiet, Chen!” Yuta rasped.

Chen’s voice rose. “look at his body, Yuta! He’s gone!”

“What did you do!?” Yuta swung his head around, his nostrils flaring, his eyes brimming with tears.

Chen’s eyes widened as his face changed to rage. “You think I’d kill my own fucking brother!?”

Yuta’s voice lowered. “I don’t know what you’re capable of.”

In response, Chen pointed at Kang’s dead body. "I would never hurt my brother.”

Yuta’s gaze darkened. “Do you expect me to believe that after your betrayal?” He points down to Kang’s body. “This was your doing, Chen. Kang’s dead because of you. Everything is your fucking fault!”

“I had nothing to do with this!”

“First father and now Kang. What else will you take from me today, brother?” Yuta asked while looking at me.

Silence.

I inspected Kang's body and around the area and gasped. On the floor, next to the toppled over table were three needles. Alarmed, I turn over Kang's body and gasp when I see his eyes wide open, his pupils dilated, his blue coloured lips and the foam at his mouth. I then gently roll the sleeves up his arms and immediately see two puncture marks.

I released his arms, lowered my head and sigh in vanquish. "He overdosed."

I point to Kang's arms, his face and the needles in the floor and both brothers begin to grieve at their loss. Chen threw back his head and releases a painful groan. "I knew this would happen. I fucking knew it! Why couldn't that punk just listen to me!? All those times I warned him of how dangerous drugs can be, and yet he still took them. I knew he'd die like this."

Chen storms out of the room, slamming the door behind him, leaving me alone with Yuta.

When I think this day couldn't possibly go worse, I'm proven wrong when I see something beyond imaginable. It wasn't the sight of Kang's dead body that brought me to my knees and a tear to my eyes, but it was the sight of the woman lying next to him. Seeing her, lying still tugged at my heartstrings

"No!" I whimpered as I held my head in my hands.

Lying motionless next to Kang and holding his hand

was Shuang. I took her frozen hand in mine, closed my eyes and shook my head in defeat.

"Is that Shuang?" Yuta asks softly.

I nod.

"Is she dead?"

I nod again.

"What happened to her?"

Shaken, I opened my eyes, examined her body and immediately saw the hole in the side of her head, and the gun lying right next to her hand. Suicide.

"She went with him." I whisper, my voice trembling.

Yuta reached up to Kang's face and with his fingers, gently closed his little brother's eyes. The sweet gesture broke my heart. Yuta remained by his brother's side until he comes to a stand. He bowed in silence and left the room without sparing a glance at me.

Now alone, I took a long lasting look at both bodies, paid my respects and left silently.

As soon as I closed the door, my eyes seek out Chen who was standing with his head lowered and his arm outstretched to the wall in front of him, completely lost in thought. Yuta was nowhere in sight.

Just as I made my way over to console Chen, an arm

unexpectedly comes around my neck, pulling me back into a chest. A grunt leaves my mouth, drawing everybody's attention at me. Next thing I know, a sharp object slices into my skin, instantly making me still. Chen takes a step forward but stops when he sees the blood trailing down my neck. He looks from me to her. "Ling?"

Ling.

I made a noise of disgust at the back of my throat, causing her to pierce the sharp object into me harder. "What? Did you forget about me?"

I scoffed. "Who could forget a back-stabbing bitch like you?"

She growled in response. "Be quiet!"

"Ling, let her go right now!" Chen demanded.

She whimpered in response. "No."

"Ling!" Chen yelled her name, causing her to shrink back in fear.

I felt her shaking her head behind me. If I release her, you'll kill me."

Chen dropped his gun to the floor and raised both of his hands. "I won't, I promise."

She whimpered again. "But I did something unforgivable."

Chen exhaled. “It’s alright, Ling. We all make mistakes.”

Was he forgiving her right now? She’s the reason why we’re in this mess in the first place.

“But...” Ling stuttered.

Chen looked pleadingly at her. “You have my word. Now, let her go. Please, Ling.”

But she didn't.

“Ling?”

“Just answer me one thing before I let her go.”

Chen nodded. “Anything.”

A pause.

“Ling...”

“That night, when I confessed my feelings to you, you said that the reason why you couldn’t reciprocate those feelings for me was because you already loved somebody else. Do you remember that night?”

“Of course, I remember.”

Her grip on me tightened. “Is she the one? The one who has your heart?”

Chen tensed his jaw but remains silent.

“Well?” Her voice was almost a whisper.

"You really want to know?"

She nodded her head repeatedly. "Please."

Another pause.

"Answer me!" Ling wailed

Chen mets my eyes and smiled softly. "Yes. She's the one."

My eyes widened in shock as I hear her gasp behind me, "Chen...?"

"I'm sorry, Ling." Chen murmured. "But it's always been her."

Her whole entire body begins to shudder in anger. Not knowing whether she'll slit my throat or throw the sharp object at Chen, I swirled around in her arms just as she lowered the knife and stabbed me in the abdomen. I hear a blood-curdling roar from behind me.

Chen.

My world explodes with pain as it's shoved deep inside of me. I cry as she slowly takes the knife out and inspects it.

"I thought you were my friend." I seethed.

"You were until you stole the man I love away from me." Ling cried.

I bring my eyes slowly up to meet hers and glare at

her. She looks back me, her face drenched with tears. "I didn't want things to end this way between you and I."

"Too fucking late for that." I snarled.

With all the strength I could muster, I snatched the knife away from her, placed it against her jugular and without a moment's hesitation, performed the killing blow. She looked at me with wide eyes as blood poured down her front. She crumpled to the floor.

Dead.

It's silent around us except for my pained grunts. I clutched my stomach and made my way over to a very pale Chen, only to crumple forward into his arms. He caught me and cradled me in his arms.

He took in my appearance and shakes his head in sorrow. "What the hell were you thinking?"

I struggled with my words. "I don't know."

He pressed down on my abdomen. The pain was beyond anything I'd ever experienced before. "I'm so sorry."

I do my best to grin. "You should be. I just saved your ass."

My once white bikini was now blood red. I looked down at my heavily injured body and exhale. "Chen?"

"Yes?"

"I don't think I'm going to make it."

Chen's brows furrowed. "Don't you dare say that, you hear me? You will make it."

I whimpered. "But I feel so weak."

And I hated feeling weak above anything else.

He cupped my cheek. "Just keeping looking at me."

I stared into his eyes and smiled. "I am looking at you."

He breaks into a grin, satisfied with my words.

"Chen?"

"Yes, Maggie?"

"Is it over?" I asked, looking side to side.

Chen looked around his surroundings then back at me. "Do you know what? I think it is."

His words brought a smile to my face. "Good."

"Maggie?"

"Yes?"

"Don't ever do something like that again, do you understand?"

I nodded, my eyes beginning to close on their own. "Okay."

"Maggie?"

“I promise.” I whispered.

“Maggie, look at me.” Chen growled.

“I promise.” I repeated.

His voice rises. “Maggie!”

“I...”

“No!”

The sound of police sirens in the distance was the last thing I heard before everything went black.

Chapter 18

Chen

I couldn’t believe it.

We’d done it.

It was over.

I couldn’t put it into words how relieved I was when we’d boarded that plane together, and took off into the sky, heading for America. Maggie had been out for the duration of the flight, getting treated for her wounds. She had yet to wake up and see where we were. I couldn't wait to see the look on her face when she realized we’d succeeded.

I had not left her side. Not even as the cops showed up, and collected Maggie and I from the villa and escorted us both to the private hanger. At any cost, I refused to let her out of my sight.

Now that Maggie was free, her family was no longer my responsibility. There was no other reason for me to stick around, but looking down at her seated next to me, I knew deep down that I wouldn’t be able to leave her alone. But after everything my family and I had put her through, I wouldn’t blame her if she didn’t want anything to do with me. The problem was, I wanted to be close to her, and the thought of never being able to see her again made me fucking miserable.

I looked down at her to see her sleeping peacefully and smiled. This was probably the only time she'd had a good night's sleep. She must've felt my gaze on her because she slowly opened her eyes and began to stir.

"Sorry. Did I wake you?" I whispered.

She shook her head.

"Did you sleep well?"

She smiled a small smile. "Best sleep I've had in a while."

A pause.

"You were beginning to make me worry. You were out for a long time."

"I was?"

I nodded, only to eye her abdomen. "Are you in pain?"

At that, she hisses in pain and clutched her stomach. "Ouch."

"Wait here, I'll get the doctor." I shoved myself out of the chair, and looked around for the doctor on board, but Maggie grabbed my hand and pulled me back down into the chair. "Don't. I'm okay."

I frowned. “But you’re hurting.”

Maggie waved me off. “I’m fine. Really. Don’t make a fuss and just sit with me.”

I didn’t need to be told twice.

“Where are we?” She asked dazedly.

Even though she looked exhausted, she still looked beautiful.

“Where do you think?” I motioned out the plane window.

With shaken arms, she turned herself in the chair and looked out of the window. She said nothing for a few seconds then covered her mouth with a gasp.

“You’re going home.” I said happily.

She leant closer into the window, her nose practically touching the glass. “Is this real? Is this a dream?”

I shook my head even though she couldn't see me. “You’re not dreaming. You’re going home.”

She turned back to me with tears in her eyes. “We did it?”

I nodded.

At that moment, her whole body began to shake as she brought her hands up to cover her face, bawling her eyes out.

I reached out and touched her cheek, and cupped it in my hand. I wiped some of her tears away and held her close against my chest. I was surprised she didn't pull away as I feared she might. Maggie wasn't the touchy-feely type.

“I can't believe it.” She murmured quietly.

I chuckled. “Believe it because soon you'll be reunited with your mother.”

She pulled back, her tears already dried on her beautiful face. “Does she know I'm coming?”

“She was notified as soon as we boarded the plane. Your mother's really excited to see you.”

My heart jolted as I saw her smile with joy. After everything she'd been through, she still managed to smile. Even after all the hardships she'd had to endure because of my disgraceful family.

She straightened her back and looked around the plane, a frown forming on her. “Where's Yuta?”

I said nothing because I didn't know how to tell her what had happened to my brother.

Maggie cocked her head to the side. “Chen?”

I sighed. “He's back in Hong Kong.”

Her frown deepened. “But he escaped with us.”

“That he did, but that's where our ties with him

ended.”

Maggie shook her head. “I don’t understand.”

H exhaled sharply. “Look, forget about him.”

"Wait." She gasped. “Is he dead?”

“No."

"Then, where is..."

I cut her off. "He’s in prison.”

Her eyes widened. “What? Why?” She spluttered.

I tear my eyes away from her and open and close my hands in tight fists as I remember what I’d done. “I made a deal. With the cops.”

“A...deal?”

I made a noise in the back of my throat in confirmation. “I made a call the night before our escape and made a deal that if I turned over Yuta to the cops and brought down my father’s empire, I’d tell them of our whereabouts and help with our escape. Out of the four of us, they wanted Li Wei and Kang the most because of all the illegal shit they’ve done, but considering both of them died, I had to give them somebody else."

"Yuta." She whispered.

I nodded.

“And why didn’t they take you?” She asked.

I shrugged. “I was their informant. And now I'm the only person who can bring my father’s entire empire down, which is what everybody fucking wants.”

Maggie nodded. “With Yuta gone, you’re the only son who can inherit all your father’s businesses.”

“Every single one of his organizations will go to me, and if I’m lucky, none of my father’s business partners know what happened yesterday or about my betrayal. That way I can shut down everything my father’s built without raising any suspicion.”

She scoffed. “Trust me, they’re going to want to know why you’re doing such a thing.”

That I knew.

My voice hardened. “They don’t have the right to ask. When you’re the Dragon Head, you answer to nobody. Doesn’t matter who you are or how old you are.”

A pause.

She grimaced at the harshness of my voice and asked. “Still, they’ll want to know what happened to them. You do realize that, right?”

“I do.” I grinned maliciously. “But by then, It’ll be too late and every single one of Li Wei’s business partners will be rotting in a cell.”

And when I mean rotting, I meant it literally.

"So will...Yuta." She uttered.

"He'll be fine, and besides, it's the best place for him to be."

I looked at her to see her eyes open wide. "But why, Chen? Why do that to your brother?"

After everything we'd just talked about, the first thing she mentioned...is him.

"I'd rather see him behind bars than dead. Look, I know he's done a lot of bad shit in the past, and he's not exactly an angel, but he's still my brother."

She gazed at me with a blank look on her face.

"And anyway, since when did you care about my brother?"

"I don't..."

I cut her off. "After everything he's done to you, you still care?"

"No..."

"Even after what he did to your father?"

She gasped as she looked at me in horror. "Chen, don't. Just don't."

"I'm sorry." I reached out to her, but she recoiled back, her brows furrowed and her eyes clenched shut. "Just don't talk about him with me. Not yet. I'm not ready."

I nodded at her request and watched as her eyes filled with moisture. I could do nothing but sit next to her, searching for words to comfort her with, but I didn't think I could say anything that would make her feel better. I had overstepped again just because of my jealousy. I bit my tongue and cursed for my outburst.

Throughout the rest of the flight, Maggie refused to look at me or speak to me. Did the feeling of triumph supposed to feel like this?

Maggie

I hadn't realized that I'd drifted off to sleep until somebody woke me up with a gentle tap to my thigh.

Chen.

What he told me as I was waking up brought butterflies into my stomach. The reason? Because we were landing and that only meant one thing.

I was home. Home.

Something I never thought I'd hear myself saying. Especially after losing dad. I'd lost hope and was beginning to accept my new life as a whore until my knight in shining armour appeared and rescued me.

Ugh.

What happened to you, Maggie?

****

The cool, evening breeze was a welcoming touch as I took my first steps out of the plane. I stopped for a couple of seconds and took it all in. Seeing the all too familiar city landscapes and landmarks brought a tear to my eye.

God, I'd missed this.

Somebody cleared their throat behind me, waking me up from my stupor.

Chen.

"Are you okay?" He asked.

Without looking back or saying anything to Chen, I just nodded and continued walking.

As soon as my feet touched the ground, a police officer approached Chen with a huge smile on his face. "Well done, sir. Very well done."

"Officer Johnson?"

"Yes." He took Chen's hand and shook it with both of his. "Thank you so much for bringing her back."

Chen smiled back at the officer. "It was my pleasure,

officer."

The officer turned his gaze to me and held out his hand to me. "Maggie?"

I nodded as I took his hand. "Hi."

"Welcome home." He said shaking my hand.

I took my hand away and avoided any kind of eye contact with anybody as my eyes began to tear up from his kind words. I wiped out my eyes as I tensed my jaw.

I used to be so tough, but now I was anything but. I was a mess.

"Has her mother arrived?" Chen asked the officer.

"She's here. Since she heard that her daughter was coming home, she has not left the airport."

My heart began to beat erratically inside my chest at the thought of my mother waiting for me. She was here, and soon I was going to see her with my very own eyes.

I looked up at Chen with tears in my eyes, while also trying to control my breathing. He gives me a heartwarming smile. "Did you hear that? She's here."

I could only bring myself to nod.

He took my hand and gently ran his thumb back and forth over the top. "You'll be fine, trust me."

I sighed. “I really want to see her, but I’m scared.”

He nodded in understanding. "I know."

My eyes widened in panic. “What am I supposed to say to her? About dad? About everything?”

He placed his hands on my shoulders and squeezed them reassuringly. “You only say what you want to say, Maggie. And besides, I think the only thing your mother wants to do with you is hold you in her arms, not ask questions about what happened to you in Hong Kong.”

Suddenly a door leading out to the private hanger bursts open and a familiar figure comes sprinting towards me, yelling my name at the top of her voice.

My heart grows twice its size at the sound of her voice, and before knowing it, my legs are running towards her. I must’ve been running like the wind because my legs were beginning to ache. But I don’t stop until I’m in her arms. The moment I feel her touch, sobs begin to erupt from my chest.

“*Eomeoni*!” **(Mother)** I wailed over and over into her shoulder.

Both of our cries drown out the noise surrounding us in the airport. Here, at this moment only the two of us existed. Nobody else. Just us.

“My baby!” My mother cries as she presses her face

against mine, kissing my soaking wet cheeks repeatedly, whispering comforting words and thank yous.

“I knew you were alive. I just knew it!”

She pulled me harder to her chest, squeezing me so tight I was struggling to breathe. She pulls me back, to get a good look at my face then smiles lovingly at me. “It’s all over now, darling. You’re safe now.”

Another sob bursts from my chest. “I missed you so much.”

She takes my face in both of her hands, her voice trembling. “I missed you too."

My mother’s head falls onto my shoulder, and the two of us hold each other in content, blessed by the fact that we were in each other’s arms once again.

“What happened wasn’t your fault, do you hear me?”

I nodded.

“Don’t blame yourself.”

I nodded again because it’s the only thing I could do.

She pulled away and held my hand tightly in hers and approached Chen, whose eyes were red-rimmed. When his eyes meet mine, he smiled a small smile.

As we get closer to him, he bowed politely to my mother. She tuts and brings him up to stand straight. “I should be bowing to you."

A single tear trails down Chen's cheek.

She cups Chen's cheek with her free hand and wipes away the tears. "Thank you so much for everything you've done for my daughter. I can't thank you enough."

"It was an honour. I'd do it again in a heartbeat."

She released my hand and crushed Chen to her chest, crying into his shoulder how grateful she was for bringing me back.

Looking at Chen makes me think of my time in captivity and our moments together. All along, he knew who I was and who my family was, and yet he still continued to be my protector.

Chen was truly my saviour.

He'd sacrificed so much to keep me alive. I owed him my life.

Looking back, I wasn't the same girl like the one on the pier that night. I wasn't the strong, fearful girl I thought I was. Now, I was the complete opposite. But that hellhole of a place is to blame. That place has completely ruined me. I didn't know it at the time, but now I do. I entered that villa with one goal in mind – to escape, but instead, it resulted in my father getting killed because of my disobedience. He died because of me. I know what I've done, and I'll never forgive myself for that. I'm going to have to live with it for the rest of my life. They say it wasn't my fault, but it is. Everything was my fault.

I cleared my throat. "*Eomeoni*, **(Mother)** could you give us a minute?"

She pulled away from Chen, looked at us both with a smile then left.

I watched my mother in panic, not wanting her to leave my sight, but I breathe a sigh of relief when I see her speaking to the police officers who were only a couple of steps away from me.

Chen chuckling brings me to attention. "She won't go far now that you're back. She'll stick to you like glue."

I wiped both of my eyes and lowered my head in embarrassment.

"Come here." Chen whispered softly, opening his arms wide for me.

Without hesitation, I walked into them and wrapped my arms tight around his back, crushing him to my chest. "You're the strongest woman I know, do you know that? You've been through hell and back and yet you still manage to break a smile."

"I'm not smiling on the inside." I murmured.

Chen sighed. "You'll heal in time, and when you do

you'll look back at this moment and berate yourself for being a pussy."

"Probably." I snicker as he pulls away.

"Maggie, you deserve to be happy after what my family's put you through. I can't tell you how sorry I am. But you don't need to worry anymore, you're safe now. Nobody can touch you now."

I nod.

"I'll drop by and see you tomorrow, okay?" He whispered.

I nodded again but stopped when I realized he was leaving me. The thought of him leaving me leaves me feeling a little unsettled, but I had to keep reminding myself that I was safe now. I was home, back with my mother. The place where I wanted to be the most.

"Maggie?"

"Yeah?"

"Wait for me." He said, the smile now disappeared from his face.

I nodded my head, watched him leave and wished that tomorrow was here already.

But he never showed.

Epilogue

Maggie

One month later...

I wiped the sweat from my forehead and addressed the room full of students. "Class dismissed. Great session everybody and I'll see you all next week."

I smiled politely as they bowed to me in unison and left for the changing rooms.

Another day is done.

The moment I'm left alone, the smile instantly vanishes from my face and misery follows soon after.

I loved the distraction teaching provided. Keeping my mind busy was all that mattered, but it was hard because now all I kept thinking about was...the small human growing inside of me. I was a month along already, and yet I still had no idea who the father was.

Was it Chen's...or was it *his*? The man who I dared not mention.

A month had gone by since the horrid events, and yet I was still being treated like a delicate flower. Throughout the last month, my mother had never left my side. She never let me out of her sight. Even when

I needed to go to the bathroom, she stayed outside the door, waiting for me to return.

In a word, it had been hell.

People said that when you experience something traumatic... you came out stronger and a lot wiser. It sounded a lot like bullshit to me. Every single night for the past month, I'd woken up in the middle of the night, with tears in my eyes and body completely drenched in sweat. Only recently had I begun to sleep better. I didn't think I would ever recover from this nightmare, but that was when I found comfort in teaching. Teaching the art of self-defence against cruel people. People like Li Wei. I wanted people to be aware that men like Li Wei were out there, waiting for their next target. I wanted people to be prepared to stand up for themselves when they needed to because the last thing I wanted was for somebody to go through what I did, but now I couldn't do that because I was pregnant.

Somebody up there had it in for me.

I was brought back to reality when the door to the changing room opened. I smiled and waved as the students left the changing rooms and filtered out towards the street.

With a sigh, I grabbed my water bottle and towel and headed to my own changing room when the door to the dojo opened.

I tied my mahogany hair into a ponytail and addressed the latecomer. "Self-defense sessions have finished for the day. Our next session is Saturday if you'd like to join the class."

"I don't want to join." A voice said amusingly.

That voice! It brings me to a sudden halt, but I shook it off and continued on my way.

I heard the person scoff. "You're still mad at me for not coming to see you?"

Again, I stopped in my tracks and frowned.

No, it couldn't be...

It wasn't him. It couldn't be. My mind was playing tricks on me. Like it did every day. Ever since he left, I hadn't stopped imagining his voice. It all started on the day he was supposed to come and see me but never showed. Ever since that day, he was all I thought about.

"You look good. Really good."

I swirled around only to come face to face with Chen. I stared wide-eyed at him and shrieked. "Chen? What the hell are you doing here!?"

He scrunched up his face. "Is this a bad time?" He pointed back to the door. "Should I go?"

"You've got some balls showing up here after asking me to wait for you and not having the decency to show up."

He shrugged. "I'm not good with goodbyes."

"That's all you have to say for yourself?"

"Well, what do you want to hear?" Chen asked.

"How about an apology for standing me up?"

A pause.

His brows rise. "Did you wait for me?"

I scoffed. "I waited for you every single fucking day and yet you never showed up."

He was silent for a few seconds then shook his head. "I didn't know you'd wait this long."

I lowered my head and exhale. "Yeah, well I did..."

Another pause.

Chen cleared his throat. "I'm sorry, but I had some loose ends to take care of."

"Bringing down your father's empire?" I asked, looking back up at him.

He nodded. "It's over. Everything Li Wei's worked for, it's all gone. All of his businesses partners are either dead or in prison, and I've inherited all of his money. Life is good. No, life is fucking great."

"And all of that took you a whole month?"

He chuckled. "No, I've been keeping a close eye on my brother."

Ah, Yuta.

My mind had wandered over to the oldest Jinyoung, but almost every time I thought of him, I shut it down.

"How...?" I stuttered.

"Is he?" He finished for me.

I nod.

"Good, I think." I look at Chen to see him with a faraway look in his eyes. "I see him every single day and he's still mad at me for what I did, but he knows prison is the best place for him. I mean, he's got his own cell and a TV. What more could he want? Plus he gets to grill at me every time he sees me, so I'd say he's doing okay."

"Wait, how come you see him every day?" I ask.

"I work as a prison guard. It's how I'm keeping an eye on him. To see if he behaves."

Unbelievable.

After all the horrid things Yuta had done to him, he still cared for his big brother.

Chen looked around the room. "I didn't know you were into teaching?"

I tutted. "Yeah, well there's a lot you don't know

about me or what I've been up to considering you've been awol."

"Maggie..."

I cut him off. "Look, if you're here to ask for forgiveness, I suggest you walk on out of here."

"But..."

My voice rised. "You've pissed me off."

He smiled. "Then, how about I make it up to you?"

"How?"

"Want to grab some coffee with me?"

I frowned. "Are you asking me out?"

"Maybe." Chen opens the door, holding it open for me. "What are you going to do about it?"

I wanted to tease him for standing me up, but I'd waited long enough, and I wasn't one to wait.

I sighed. "I want to say rain-check, but I don't have the patience to wait for you, so let's go. Oh, and you're paying."

He grins wickedly at me. "Fine by me, but only if you pay for dinner?"

I halted my movements and glared at him. "You're joking right?"

"Of course, I am, I'm not that mean. Plus, I've got a

lot to make up for."

I cup his cheek and tap it at the last second. "That you do."

As I walked out the door, I dropped the smile and clutched my stomach tightly.

What in the fuck was I going to do?